Books by Mark Cheverton

The Gameknight999 Series
*Invasion of the Overworld*
*Battle for the Nether*
*Confronting the Dragon*

The Mystery of Herobrine Series: A Gameknight999 Adventure
*Trouble in Zombie-town*
*The Jungle Temple Oracle*
*Last Stand on the Ocean Shore*

Herobrine Reborn Series: A Gameknight999 Adventure
*Saving Crafter*
*The Destruction of the Overworld*
*Gameknight999 vs. Herobrine*

Herobrine's Revenge Series: A Gameknight999 Adventure
*The Phantom Virus*
*Overworld in Flames*
*System Overload*

The Birth of Herobrine: A Gameknight999 Adventure
*The Great Zombie Invasion*
*Attack of the Shadow-Crafters*
*Herobrine's War (Coming Soon!)*

The Mystery of Entity303: A Gameknight999 Adventure
*Terrors of the Forest (Coming soon!)*
*Monsters in the Mist (Coming soon!)*
*Mission to the Moon (Coming soon!)*

*The Gameknight999 Box Set*
*The Gameknight999 vs. Herobrine Box Set*

The Algae Voices of Azule Series
*Algae Voices of Azule*
*Finding Home*
*Finding the Lost*

AN UNOFFICIAL NOVEL

# ATTACK OF THE SHADOW-CRAFTERS

## THE BIRTH OF HEROBRINE
### BOOK TWO
### <<< A GAMEKNIGHT999 ADVENTURE >>>

AN UNOFFICIAL MINECRAFTER'S ADVENTURE

# MARK CHEVERTON

SKY PONY PRESS
NEW YORK

Copyright © 2016 by Mark Cheverton

Minecraft® is a registered trademark of Notch Development AB

The Minecraft game is copyright © Mojang AB

Sky Pony Press books may be purchased in bulk at special discounts for sales promotion, corporate gifts, fund-raising, or educational purposes. Special editions can also be created to specifications. For details, contact the Special Sales Department, Sky Pony Press, 307 West 36th Street, 11th Floor, New York, NY 10018 or info@ skyhorsepublishing.com.

Sky Pony® is a registered trademark of Skyhorse Publishing, Inc.®, a Delaware corporation.

Visit our website at www.skyponypress.com.

10 9 8 7 6 5 4 3 2

Library of Congress Cataloging-in-Publication Data is available on file.

Cover design by Owen Corrigan
Cover artwork by Thomas Frick
Technical consultant: Gameknight999

Print ISBN: 978-1-5107-0995-9
Ebook ISBN: 978-1-5107-1000-9

Printed in Canada

# ACKNOWLEDGMENTS

I'd like to thank my family for all their support through the writing of this book. As always, they are very understanding of my irrational terror when I'm facing the blank page at the beginning of the writing process. They listen to my rantings when I say I can't possibly get the next book written before deadline, then laugh at me when I finish ahead of schedule. My wife, son, and mother-in-law are the greatest support network I could ever ask for.

# NOTE FROM THE AUTHOR

For some reason, *Attack of the Shadow-Crafters* seemed the most difficult book to write so far. I'm betting I say this every time, but this time I mean it. I thought for sure that I couldn't come up with anything decent for all of you to read and figured this was the end of my creative streak. But then something clicked, and this book flowed from my fingers and into my computer almost faster than I could type. I am really excited about this story and hope you feel the same as I do about it. It could possibly be the best of the Gameknight999 adventures.

This time around, I did something different, and I think it made a big difference. Before writing, I built some of the scenes that were important to the story, specifically Dragon's Teeth, on the Gameknight999 Minecraft server. It really helped me not only to get the story right but also to write better descriptions of the environment. I hope you can perfectly visualize the rocky spires of Dragon's Teeth while you read, and I hope that when you're done, you go check them out on the server to see if they match up to what you'd imagined. Directions on how to find the book warps are listed at the end of this book, along with the Minecraft seeds.

We are adding lots of new games to the Gameknight999 Minecraft server, some of them with references to the books. See if you can find all of them! Hopefully, with quadbamber's help (you can find him as LBEGaming on Youtube) we'll be adding some custom-developed games that will involve some of the battles in the books. Fingers crossed, you'll soon be able to find the king of the Endermen, Erebus, or the spider queen, or Oxus, the creeper king, lurking around on the server. Maybe they will give you a present if you can destroy them. Keep your eyes peeled for their arrival. You can find information about the server, including the IP address, at www.gameknight999. com. And as always, look for Gameknight999 and me, Monkeypants_271 out there; maybe we can do a little PVP, if you are brave enough (sorry, I'm not very good at PVP, ☺).

Keep reading, and watch out for creepers.

Mark

When you believe in yourself, accept your weaknesses as things you can improve on, and acknowledge your strengths as things to be proud of, you can become a truer version of yourself. People might accept this truer self, or they might not, but if you truly believe in yourself, then it won't matter.

# CHAPTER I

# CRAFTING OF AN OLD FRIEND

**H**erobrine was furious at the destruction of his army. That fool of a zombie king, Vo-Lok, had had the advantage in that battle in the mountain pass, and yet he had still lost . . . to a simple blacksmith. Now, the evil virus's two remaining monster kings stood at his side.

Shaikulud, the spider queen, was enraged. Her purple eyes blazed with fury as she stalked back and forth, barely able to contain her anger. She'd seen many of her spiders destroyed in the battle, all for nothing. None of them had expected the NPCs to fight as hard as they did. And when the villagers had been surrounded, the monsters had all thought the villagers would just surrender and beg for mercy. But instead, the NPCs fought harder; it made no sense.

Oxus, the creeper king, was angry as well, but for different reasons. He knew Herobrine had wasted thirty of his creepers in an experiment: throwing his green monsters at the villagers, while the creatures of smoke and flame, the blazes, ignited them with their fireballs. It hadn't been necessary. Creepers were peace-loving creatures that only detonated to save the lives of their kin, but now . . . Oxus was sure word would spread of the attack, and villagers would attack the creepers on sight.

While the remaining monster king and queen were unhappy, that was nothing compared to the anger that Herobrine felt.

"That foolish zombie king, Vo-Lok," Herobrine growled. "He had the villagers bottled up in that narrow pass, and he let them escape." His dark eyes began to glow bright with rage as he looked across the desert at the NPC army slowly heading south, away from the site of the zombie king's destruction. "We will forever call the pit where the battle was lost the Pit of Despair."

"Why?" the spider queen asked.

"Because despair was likely the last thing that idiotic zombie king experienced," Herobrine grumbled.

A robotic wheezing sound floated across the landscape; it sounded like some kind of mechanical demon gasping for breath. A handful of blazes floated over the desert sand, their internal flames flickering with instability. They were creatures Herobrine had brought to the Overworld from the Nether, in hopes they could help with the creepers . . . and they had. But now there were only a dozen or so remaining, and all were near death. Herobrine knew they needed lava to replenish their health points (HP) or they would perish. He glared at them with his harsh white eyes and they floated away, careful to stay out of reach.

Herobrine growled in frustration. He paced back and forth, his booted feet pounding the ground with anger as if he were trying to punish the land itself. He hated being trapped in this server and wanted to escape; but he knew it was likely impossible. As a virus, Herobrine could remember life in the Internet, invading servers and destroying apps, but when he'd come into Minecraft, something had happened. Somehow, he awakened all the creatures of this world, bringing them to life with his artificial intelligence software. He, too, had come to life, and along with his sentience came the frustration of feeling caged within these tiny Minecraft servers. Herobrine vowed to destroy the innocent creatures of this land; the suffering of others made his captivity feel more tolerable.

"What now, Maker?" Oxus hissed, his ignition process starting as he spoke. "You no longer have a monster army."

"Monsters are no problem," Herobrine said as he turned away. The sight of the victorious NPCs had made him sick. "I can always get more monsters; that is of no concern. But now we lack a leader. Neither of you are strong enough to command my army."

He glanced down at the spider queen.

"Shaikulud, you never fully commit," Herobrine said. "You are cautious . . . *too* cautious. I gave you too much of my intelligence during your creation."

He turned and faced the creeper king.

"And Oxus, you have too much compassion for your subjects," Herobrine said. "You treat them as if they were your children. I see it in your eyes. You will never make the hard decision to sacrifice some so that the greater goal can be achieved."

Turning away from the two monster kings, the virus slowly walked down the sandy hill on which they stood.

"You are both too weak and would never make good leaders. I must have another." He turned and glared at the two monsters. "Follow!"

Shaikulud and Oxus scurried down the large sand dune, following their Maker.

"I will craft another leader for my monster army," Herobrine explained. "While I am away, both of you will gather more troops. We'll need a huge mob of spiders and creepers to help with the attack on the villagers. We cannot let their leader, that black-smith Smithy, get away with destroying my zombie king and my army. When I return, I expect to find you with more of your kind, or one of you will be sacrificed. Do you understand?"

The two monsters just stopped and stared at him, shocked.

"I said, 'Do you understand?'" Herobrine repeated, looking away from the monsters, his eyes still burning bright with anger.

"Yes," they both replied.

"Very well," Herobrine said. "Shaikulud, you will gather your spiders, then find the villagers and their leader, Smithy, the blacksmith. Your task is simple: make them suffer. Do you understand?"

The queen of the spiders peered up at her Maker and nodded her dark, fuzzy head, her multiple eyes glowing bright purple with evil delight as her razor-sharp mandibles clicked together excitedly.

"Oxus, you will bring me more creepers. I will not accept your excuses. Bring them to me or meet you doom. Understood?"

The creeper king, with jagged bolts of red and blue lightning dancing across his green skin, nodded his head.

"Do not disappoint me . . . *either* of you."

With that threat still hanging in the air, Herobrine closed his eyes and disappeared from the desert. At the speed of thought, he teleported deep underground, materializing at the edge of a massive lava lake. At the far side of the boiling lake, he saw what looked like a short wall that held back a large body of water; it was an underground sea. Teleporting to the wall, Herobrine balled his hand into a fist and smashed the stone barrier. Instantly, the water flowed out and covered the molten stone. When the cool water touched the boiling hot stone, the two combined to form a dark, sparkling sheet of obsidian, as was expected in Minecraft.

Herobrine stepped out onto the purple sheet of stone. The heat from the dark cubes radiated upward into his boots; it made them feel magical and alive. Tiny purple crystals sparkled in the distant light from the lava on the far side of the cave, giving the black cubes just a splash of lavender.

"Perfect," the evil shadow-crafter said.

Closing his eyes, he concentrated on his inner being, on that core portion of his mind that could connect to the software that surrounded him. Because he was an artificially intelligent virus, programmed to hack into the Minecraft server, Herobrine had certain abilities; these powers formed his shadow-crafting powers.

As he concentrated on his code-altering skills, his hands glowed a pale, sickly yellow, which started at his fingertips but slowly seeped across his hands until the insipid light moved up his arms. He opened his eyes and stared down at his hands. An evil smile spread across his square face as he felt his shadow-crafting powers fill his being.

In a flash of motion, Herobrine knelt and plunged his hands into the warm obsidian, merging with the stone. Instantly, the diseased-looking pale glow oozed across the sparkling purple sheet. Reaching out, he drove his crafting powers outward until they encompassed not only the obsidian sheet on which he knelt, but also the shadowy corners of the caverns. Drawing the darkness to him, he merged the shadows with the obsidian, forming a new material never before seen in Minecraft. As he pulled more of the shadows into the creation, Herobrine crafted, using every drop of hatred for the NPCs surging through his veins.

"My creation will be as fast as a shadow following a nightmare," he mumbled to himself. "It will be a glorious creature, violent and strong and evil—perfect in every way."

Herobrine's speed and aggressive temper began to seep into his creation, but also, unknowingly, his own vanity oozed into it as well. Soon, something began to form before him.

"You will be so magnificent that nothing will dare attack you," Herobrine said, his voice echoing off the cavern walls and coming back to him on all sides. "You will stand among your enemies and none will be brave enough to even look at you." Herobrine's overwhelming confidence began to drip into the creation, giving it a self-assurance and bravery unmatched by anything else on the Minecraft servers.

With his hands glowing brighter and brighter, he shaped the material into a long, lanky shape with thin legs and narrow arms. The thing before him slowly morphed into the body of a creature, dark and sinister. Herobrine had imbued it with the sparkling teleportation powers of the obsidian, but at the same time he filled it with his own vile contempt for all of the good things in life, like happiness, or family, or . . . peace.

Once the monster was complete, Herobrine plunged his hands into the creature, driving all his viral powers into it, causing it to replicate all across the obsidian plane.

"You will replicate in the shadowy places of Minecraft, drinking in the darkness to form your lean bodies."

In the blink of an eye, there were a hundred of the dark creatures strewn all across the chamber. It was difficult to see them, for their bodies were completely black, merging with the shadows. Slowly, many of the dark monsters struggled to stand.

The one lying before Herobrine began to rise as well, but the evil shadow-crafter held it down.

"Not yet, my child," Herobrine said with a vile laugh.

Reaching into his inventory, the virus drew an iron sword and gave himself the smallest cut on his arm. But instead of flashing with damage, Herobrine allowed the lines of code that pulsed through his veins to leak out slowly. The 1's and 0's that formed Herobrine's evil, hateful personality oozed from the wound like thick red honey. In a single gloppy drop, the viral lines of code fell and landed on the dark creature before him, slowly spreading out across its skin, infecting every bit of the monster with Herobrine's hateful code and staining the shadowy monster with a dark red hue.

Satisfied, Herobrine stood and stepped back.

"Arise, my child," Herobrine said in a low voice. "I have brought you into existence solely to serve me. Now stand."

The creature before him stood on shaky legs, unsure of its new body. The other, newly-created monsters approached and looked down upon their maker, a touch of anger and vile contempt on their dark faces.

"Behold, I have crafted a new creature to serve me," Herobrine said. "You will all be called Endermen, and the one that carries the smallest sliver of my viral code will be your king."

Herobrine's eyes began to glow white, allowing him to clearly see the creatures. All but one of the Endermen were pitch black, and they had eyes that were the same purple hue as the tiny flakes of color in the obsidian. But the king of the Endermen was different. Instead of deep purple, this creature had bright crimson eyes that seemed to be filled with a hatred for all living things. His skin lacked the shadowy black color. Instead, there was a dark red tint to his skin, like the color of dried blood . . . it was wonderful.

"Your king will command you in battle. Do as he says or suffer a punishment that will make you wish you had never been created."

The Endermen moved closer. Some of them teleported back and forth across the chamber, testing their new capabilities.

"Maker," one of the Endermen said in a high-pitched screech. "What do we do, and what do we call our king?"

"Hmmm," Herobrine mused, then a smile spread across his face. "You will go forth and find my enemy, the blacksmith Smithy. You will make him suffer and remind him of my wrath. Tell him that I'm coming for him and there is no place he can hide."

"But what of our king?" another asked. "What do we call him?"

"His name will be that of an ancient demon that I remember from my life before arriving in Minecraft."

The Endermen moved closer, anxious to hear the name.

"Your king will be the tip of the spear," Herobrine said. "He will lead my forces against the pathetic NPCs until they are all destroyed. He will show no mercy, and be relentless as he punishes those that resist me."

He glared at the creatures in the room, his eyes glowing with a harsh brightness that made the Endermen look away when his gaze fell on them. But the king of the Endermen did not look away. He stood tall, feeling power and hatred surge through him.

"Your king," Herobrine continued, "will be called Erebus."

The Enderman king let out a spine-tingling screech that cut through Minecraft like a rusty razorblade, leaving in its wake only pain and fear.

# CHAPTER 2
# SEARCHING FOR SAFETY

ameknight999 scanned the desert, looking for monsters. Reaching up, he adjusted the iron helmet that sat on his square head, hiding his face from the other villagers. It was very heavy, more for the responsibility it represented than just its weight.

*How did I get in this mess?* he thought.

He was trapped far in Minecraft's past, having used his father's invention, the Digitizer, to enter this digital landscape, his entire being sent *into* the game. But something had gotten messed up, and he'd accidentally been transported into the past, to the time of Minecraft's Great Zombie Invasion. Now he was stuck in the middle of a war, trying to help the villagers, or NPCs (non-playable characters) defend themselves against an army of monsters.

They had just finished the battle led by Herobrine's zombie king, Vo-Lok, where they had defeated him in the desert. They'd escaped the monsters' trap in the narrow pass that cut through the mountains and pushed the army of villains deep into the desert, bombarding them with blocks of TNT until all the zombies and skeletons were destroyed. Now, a gigantic hole extended all the way down to bedrock and marked the place where the battle had been won. But the cost had been great. Many lives were lost amongst the NPCs, and even more were wounded.

"We need to find a place to rest and heal," Fencer said.

Gameknight moved to his friend's side and whispered in his ear.

"You think anyone knows I'm not Smithy?" he asked.

During the terrible battle, the villagers' leader, a blacksmith named Smithy, had been hit by multiple arrows and fell from the fortified wall. In the chaos, no one had noticed that Fencer and Gameknight had rushed to Smithy's side, only to find him gravely wounded. Smithy died, but with his final breaths he had commanded Gameknight to take his armor and helmet and fight in his stead. When the User-that-is-not-a-user had stood wearing the blacksmith's leather armor and iron helmet, none of the villagers had suspected the identity switch. And when he drew his two swords, the NPCs had rallied behind him, cementing Gameknight999's guise as the historic and legendary leader, Smithy of the Two-Swords.

The troops fought with renewed courage at the sight of their fearless leader battling with dual blades. They drove the monsters out into the desert, where they were eventually defeated. But now, without the confusion of battle, Gameknight was more nervous than ever that someone would notice that he wasn't actually Smithy and was only pretending to be him.

"I don't think anyone knows," Fencer said in a low voice. As far as Gameknight knew, Fencer was the only person who knew the truth; in fact, he'd been at Smithy's side with Gameknight when the NPC had died and had pushed Gameknight to take Smithy's place. "Just keep that helmet on. If you take it off, they will see that small nose of yours and instantly realize what happened."

Gameknight nodded anxiously, then scanned the crowd of villagers. He could still see the confidence that his two-sword trick had instilled in them, but he also saw a touch of fear. They were far from home, and even though they'd won the battle, Herobrine was still about, ready to cause mischief. That virus was intent on destroying all NPCs. He was pure evil.

He glanced up above him, half-expecting to see the letters spelling out his name hovering over his head. As a user, Gameknight should have had his name glowing over his head along with a server thread stretching up into the air, connecting him to the servers. But he didn't have either now, because he wasn't really logged into the game like he usually would have been. Instead, he was completely *in* the game. Gameknight could feel everything. He could feel the heat of the sun and hear the rasp of the dried shrubs that rustled in the constant east-to-west wind that always flowed across Minecraft. The dust that rode on those winds clogged his nostrils and made him thirsty. So he was a user in the game, but not really in the game; he was the User-that-is-not-a-user.

"Where's Mapper?" Gameknight shouted in a deep, baritone voice. Smithy's voice was lower than his, and in order to keep up his disguise, he would need to sound like the blacksmith as much as possible.

"Here," a scratchy voice said.

The old villager pushed his way through the crowd that was milling about on the sandy terrain. They were heading vaguely south, but with no particular destination in mind. They were just glad to not be battling any monsters.

Gameknight moved to the NPC's side.

"Is there a village nearby?" the User-that-is-not-a-user asked.

"Well, there is the village back in the savannah, but it's far from here," the old NPC said. "I don't think everyone will make it."

"I know that," Gameknight said, a little impatient. "Ahh . . . sorry," he added, shaking his head to clear it. "Isn't there anything closer?"

"I remember there being a desert village to the east, near the Great Chasm."

"'The Great Chasm'?" Gameknight asked. "What's that?"

"It's a deep ravine carved into the Overworld," the old NPC explained. "It stretches through multiple biomes and goes right through the mountains that run along the edge of the Northern Desert."

"So it will keep monsters from approaching us?" the User-that-is-not-a-user asked.

Mapper nodded, his long gray hair falling across his square face.

"Then lead the way. We'll rest there and replenish our supplies."

The army turned and headed toward the east, using the rest of the daylight to move as far as they could before nightfall.

"Oink." The sound came from behind him. Gameknight turned and found his pet pig, Wilbur, staring up at him. He looked like he was uncomfortable.

"Ahh . . . is the hot sand hurting your feet?" the User-that-is-not-a-user asked.

"Oink," the pig replied.

Bending down, Gameknight scooped up the pig and held him in his arms.

"We'll be somewhere a little more comfortable soon," he said to his companion.

"What do you think happened to Herobrine after the battle?" a young boy said next to him.

Gameknight looked down, shocked by how bright the youthful NPC's blue eyes seemed, especially next to his long, dark brown hair. The boy wore a bright yellow smock with a chocolate brown stripe that ran down the center. The likeness was unmistakable: this was Weaver, the great-uncle of his friend Crafter, that he'd left back in the future . . . or present . . . or was it the past now? It was very confusing.

Normally, when he used his father's Digitizer, it would just send Gameknight *into* the game, but a bolt of lightning had struck his house right as he activated the device, and something strange had happened . . . which had landed him here, a hundred years in the past. It was terrifying, but also exciting at the same time. He was standing next to Crafter's great-uncle, long before Crafter's parents had ever been born. He knew from Crafter that Weaver had taught him everything he knew about TNT. That knowledge had saved countless villagers in the present . . . or future . . . or . . . ugh, it was so confusing it made his head hurt. But if something happened and Weaver was killed, then there would be no one to teach Crafter how to use TNT, right? It would change the future, and possibly lead to the destruction of countless lives. Gameknight had to help these villagers with this war, and at the same time, protect the ancestors of his friends. Little Weaver here was one of the most important ones.

The young boy reached out and petted the pig.

"I don't know what happened to Herobrine," Gameknight said. "I lost sight of him when we destroyed Vo-Lok and the monster army."

"I saw him from the hilltop as I was firing the TNT cannons," Weaver said. "He was watching from a distant sand dune with the creeper king and the spider queen. They just stood there for a while, then disappeared after we were victorious."

"He likely ran away to sulk," Fencer said.

"Maybe, but you can be sure he's still out there," Gameknight said. "And he's planning something. We still need to be careful. I have no doubt Herobrine is likely preparing for another attack."

"Smithy, you're always expecting some kind of attack," one of the villagers said. Gameknight turned and saw it was Stonecutter. "Smithy, you be crazy sometimes. You're like that stranger that came to our village. Whatever happened to him?"

"I think he died in the battle," one of the other NPCs said. "Don't even remember his name."

"It's not important," Gameknight said, trying to change the subject. He knew they were talking about him. "What we need to do now is get to that desert village and take care of our wounded. Herobrine will not wait until we're healed to launch his next attack. As soon as he is ready, he'll strike. We need information so that our defense will be ready when Herobrine returns."

"Yep, you're right, Stonecutter," one of the village elders said. "Smithy be crazy alright."

The NPCs laughed as one of them slapped Gameknight on the back, almost making him trip and drop Wilbur. Quickly, the User-that-is-not-a-user reached up with one hand and grabbed his helmet so it wouldn't fall off, then continued marching with everyone else to the east and toward the distant village that still lay hidden behind the horizon.

Suddenly, a high-pitched screech rode in on the gentle breeze. Gameknight strained to listen, thinking at first that it must be his imagination, because he knew of only one creature in all of Minecraft that could make that sound. It might be his fatigue making him hear things, he thought, looking down at his arm and watching tiny little square goose bumps form and spread.

But then Wilbur glanced up at him with an expression of fear on his pink face as well; maybe the noise was real? Gameknight shuddered as a feeling of terror slithered through his soul.

# CHAPTER 3

# SPIDERS

They trudged through the desert, those that were still healthy wrapping their arms around the shoulders of the wounded. The sun hung low in the west, moving slowly toward the horizon in the late afternoon. The sky had not begun shifting from the bright blues of day to the warm red and eventual black of night, not yet. But it was coming soon, and none of the villagers wanted to be out in the open at night. Nighttime was monster time in Minecraft.

Gameknight scanned the desert with his keen eyes, searching for threats. That terrible screeching noise earlier still had him worried, though he was trying to convince himself that it was just his imagination.

*What was that?!* he thought, suddenly noticing something sharp and dangerous looking from the corner of his eye. But when he turned to face it, he found it was only a cactus, the tiny brown dried bush at his feet, rustling in the wind.

*I'm too jumpy; I have to calm down.*

"Smithy, are you OK?" Fencer asked loudly as he strode up alongside him, the NPC's eyes filled with worry. Then, when he was close enough to be out of earshot of anyone else, whispered to the User-that-is-not-a-user. "What's going on, Gameknight? The real Smithy wouldn't be jumping at the sight of desert flora."

"I know, I know . . . I just thought I heard something back a while ago and it has me a little freaked out," Gameknight replied.

"What did you hear?" the NPC asked.

"Ahh . . . well," Gameknight stammered. "I thought it sounded like an—"

"Look, a desert well!" one of the scouts suddenly shouted.

Gameknight ran up the sand dune in front of them. As he reached the crest, the next dune came into view. Sitting on its peak, a desert well stood tall, its square structure looking out of place among the flowing sea of smooth sandy mounds.

"Go check it out," the User-that-is-not-a-user said to the scout. "Take some others with you."

The scout, Runner (named for obvious reasons, Gameknight quickly realized), pointed to three others and dashed forward. He sprinted down the dune face and across the sandy desert, easily outpacing his companions. He ran so fast that he reached the structure when the other three were just beginning to climb the hill. Gameknight watched as Runner inspected the well carefully, making sure there were no traps. He then scanned the surroundings, looking for monsters, and eventually waved the rest of them forward.

"Come on, everyone, let's get some water," Gameknight said. "Those that are wounded drink first."

The army moved down the hill and crossed the hot, sandy landscape. Some of the injured had difficulty climbing the next hill and had to be helped, but most made it to the well without any difficulty.

Glancing to the west, the User-that-is-not-a-user saw the sky begin to blush a warm orange that slowly shifted to red. The boxy white clouds stayed brightly lit, standing out against the darkening sky. To the east, stars began to show their sparkling faces through the blue veil. The eastern sky was growing black, signaling the villagers to begin worrying.

Gameknight999 climbed the sand dune and approached the well. Fencer met him with a bottle of water in one hand.

"Here," his newfound friend said.

He handed the bottle over. Gameknight took it and chugged all the liquid inside. The water felt cold and refreshing as it went down his throat, cooling his body just a bit, a welcome relief to the oppressive heat of the desert.

"Thanks," the User-that-is-not-a-user replied, handing back the empty bottle. "Any idea how much farther we have to go?"

"Not sure," Fencer replied. "I think Mapper is a bit lost but doesn't want to admit it. He's certain it's to the east of here. The question is: how far?"

The land around them began to grow dark as the sun settled behind a line of hills to the west. Overhead, the black sky spread across the heavens like a blanket being drawn across the world, with holes in the covering to allow the stars to shine through. Glancing to the east, Gameknight scanned the darkening desert, looking for the village that was hidden somewhere out there in the bleak wasteland.

Tiny sparkles flicked across the sky unexpectedly. *What was that?* Gameknight thought. Fatigue pulled heavily on every muscle, especially his mind. *Am I seeing things?* But he couldn't have seen fireflies in Minecraft; they were only in modded versions of the game, like the Twilight Forest. Blinking his eyes, he gazed out into the dark landscape. There it was again, though: a group of red spots moving around in the darkness, getting closer. His tired brain attempted to process what he was seeing, but he was just too exhausted to make any sense of it.

"Fencer, you see that out there?" Gameknight said. He pointed in the direction of the red spots.

The NPC stared out into the desert, looking for what Gameknight was pointing at.

"I don't see anything," Fencer said. "But I'm pretty tired. What am I supposed to see?"

Gameknight peered into the darkness again. The spots were gone, the desert empty. Then they appeared again, but this time there were more of the red spots, a lot more of them, and they were getting closer. Suddenly, recognition hit Gameknight like a ton of bricks, filling him with renewed energy . . . and panic.

"Spider eyes . . . they're spider eyes!" the User-that-is-not-a-user exclaimed.

"What?" Fencer asked.

"Spiders are coming!" Gameknight shouted. "Everyone put your backs to the well and get ready. Wounded to the inside, swordsmen to the outside."

"We need some archers on top of the well," Fencer added. "Get up there fast."

A group of warriors placed blocks on the ground, making some rough steps, then climbed to the top of the well. Only eight of them could fit, but it was better than nothing.

"Where's Wilbur?" Gameknight said suddenly, thinking of his friend.

"Oink oink," the pig said.

"Weaver, take care of Wilbur for me," Gameknight said. "Pick him up and keep him near the well where it will be safe."

"But I was going to fight," the young boy complained.

"Just do this for me," Gameknight snapped quickly.

The NPC sighed, then scooped up the animal and moved behind the warriors.

Gameknight smiled. It would not only keep Wilbur safe, but Weaver as well. He had to keep that boy from harm's way. If he didn't, who would teach Crafter about TNT in the future?

Turning, he stared out into the desert. The villagers could all see the red, glowing eyes of the spiders now. They were approaching from the north and moving fast. Gameknight turned so he was facing the mob, then drew his two iron swords.

"We aren't afraid of a bunch of puny spiders, are we?" Gameknight said.

A feeble cheer rose from the defenders. He turned and faced the warriors.

"I know you are all tired, but this is just a probe," Gameknight said. "Herobrine is testing us, checking to see if we have any courage left after the battle with the zombie king. But I say to you: we can meet this challenge, because we are fighting not just for ourselves, but for all of Minecraft. Now, are you ready?"

"Yeah!" they cheered, half-heartedly.

"I said, 'ARE YOU READY?'"

"YEAH!" the villagers cried.

Gameknight smiled, then turned and faced the oncoming monsters. He could now see their dark, fuzzy bodies in the silvery light of the moon rising in the east. There was a dozen of the monsters—not a huge threat, but still enough to do some damage to these villagers, and Gameknight999 wasn't going to allow that to happen.

"Smithy, another group is coming from the south!" one of the archers shouted.

Gameknight glanced over his shoulder and saw another cluster of spiders approaching. Two groups . . . that was not good.

The spiders charged up the hill. Bowstrings sang as arrows streaked down at the lead monsters. The first few spiders fell under the barrage, but as soon as the next lines of attack reached the NPCs, the archers could no longer shoot without risking hitting their own.

A great crash filled the desert air when the spider claws met swords. The monsters spread out so they surrounded the villagers. Though they were outnumbered, the spiders fought as if they didn't care about their own survival. Their wicked curved claws slashed at armor, scratching the tough leather and putting small gashes in the protective coating.

Gameknight could see this fight was not going well. Their troops needed something to inspire them. Leaping forward, Gameknight landed right in the middle of the monsters. Spinning like a top, he slashed with his dual swords, tearing into the HP of multiple creatures. They tried to reach him with their claws, but his swords drove them back.

The villagers saw the insane attack by their leader and cheered. They pushed forward, attacking with renewed courage.

But more of the fuzzy monsters emerged from the desert, adding their claws to the battle. There were now at least thirty of them, and the villagers behind Gameknight were all tired. They needed a trick to get out of this battle and drive the spiders away.

And suddenly, the solution popped into Gameknight's head: creepers.

"Weaver, you remember that trick we did with the creepers at the village?" Gameknight shouted as he destroyed a spider.

"Sure do," shouted the young boy.

"Do it . . . now!"

The User-that-is-not-a-user fought his way back to the villagers, then slashed at every monster that came near. He glanced left and right, looking for villagers that needed help. One of them, a builder, shouted out in pain. Gameknight streaked to his side and charged at the monster before him. The spider saw him in the blacksmith's armor and helmet, and the creature's eyes glowed bright with excitement. Its claws slashed at Gameknight, first bouncing off his iron helmet, then striking at his chest. The User-that-is-not-a-user blocked the attack with his left blade, then struck the beast with his right. It screamed in pain and tried to attack, but Builder was there to drive the attack home. After two more hits, the monster disappeared, a look of fear and despair on its hideous face.

"Everyone, back up!" Weaver yelled.

The villagers scooted back as far as they could. A group of young NPCs then stepped forward and dumped water on the ground before them. The liquid spread, pushing the spiders back down the hill.

"Everyone, use your bows!" Gameknight shouted.

In an instant, the warriors put away their swords and pulled out their bows. The desert came alive with the twanging of bowstrings as the villagers fired upon the creatures. Struggling against the watery flow, the spiders tried to move forward and reach the NPCs, but the young kids were adding more water to the defenses every second, pushing the spiders a little farther down the hill each time.

"Keep firing!" Fencer shouted.

Gameknight fired three quick shots, like his friend Hunter from the future had taught him. The trio of projectiles struck a spider, one after the other, and brought its HP to zero. But before the monster disappeared, Gameknight999 was already aiming at another monster. In minutes, the villagers had cleared the desert of spiders save for one that stood far away, out of range.

"Herobrine ssssendsss a messssage," the spider hissed loudly.

The monster had purple eyes that glowed bright in the darkness. They reminded Gameknight of the eyes on the Ender Dragon, purple and evil. Instantly, he recognized the beast; it was Shaikulud, the queen of the spiders.

"Tell your master we are not afraid!" Gameknight shouted back.

The spider laughed.

"Herobrine wantssss you to know, he issss coming for you," the spider queen said. "He will desssstroy all of you, then do the ssssame to all the villlagessss in the Overworld. Ssssoon thissss land will belong to the monssssterssss."

Before Gameknight could reply, Shaikulud turned and scurried off into the desert.

"Friend of yours, Smithy?" Fencer asked.

Some of the NPCs laughed.

"That's Shaikulud, the spider queen," Gameknight said. "And yes, I've encountered her before."

"When?" someone asked.

"It was . . . err . . . a long time from now, I mean, ago," he stammered.

"Whenever it was, I think I'd rather not meet her again," Fencer added quickly, frowning at Gameknight.

"Me, too," Gameknight agreed. "Let's move out and get to that desert village."

The NPCs placed blocks of sand on the watery flow, cutting off the streams and allowing them to continue to the east. They then moved with renewed haste, running through the desert toward the village they all hoped was there.

# CHAPTER 4

# DESERT VILLAGE

The army moved quickly, eyes watching the dark terrain with care. Their wounded were kept at the center of the formation. Gameknight placed a ring of swordsmen around them, then a ring of archers on the outside. If they spotted any monsters, the archers would slow them down as the swordsmen moved into position; that was the hope, anyway.

They continued east, with the tall line of mountains and extreme hills to their right and the open desert on their left. Gameknight was at the head of the formation, taking the path that would be the easiest on the wounded. As a result, he wove around dunes and clusters of cactuses, their sharp, pointed spines poking anyone that strayed too close.

Nothing stirred in the desert as they made their trek toward the unseen village in the distance. Their surroundings seemed unusually quiet, and that worried everyone. The gentle east-to-west wind blew constantly against their backs, coating the back of their armor with dust. Occasionally, one of the brown, dried bushes would rustle in the breeze, making a sound that reminded Gameknight of a rattlesnake, though he didn't mention it to the others; they would have no idea what a snake even was.

The tension in the air was palpable. Their nerves and their courage were stretched tight to the point of breaking. If another group of monsters fell on them, it would likely shatter the resolution of the army, maybe permanently.

*We have to get to the desert village, or everything could be lost,* Gameknight thought.

"Don't worry, we'll get there," Fencer said, as if the User-that-is-not-a-user had been speaking out loud.

"How could you tell that I was worried?" Gameknight asked.

"Because every muscle in your body is clenched, and you walk stiff, like an iron golem," the NPC replied with a smile.

"I think maybe we should tell them all the truth about Smithy, before things get too far out of control," Gameknight whispered.

"Are you kidding?" Fencer growled in a low voice. "The courage of this army is hanging on by a thread. It would destroy them. Don't worry, when the time is right, we'll come clean. But for now, you have to keep on pretending to be Smithy until all this settles down a bit."

Gameknight sighed.

"Fine," the User-that-is-not-a-user replied reluctantly.

Suddenly, Fencer shouted out loud, making him jump.

"There it is!"

Gameknight looked where Fencer was pointing. Off to the right, the soft yellow glow of torches lit the desert as sandstone houses came into view. Light from the open windows spilled out onto the sands and bathed the desert with a welcoming illumination that eased many fears. To everyone around him, it seemed like paradise.

"Come on, everyone, we made it!" the User-that-is-not-a-user shouted.

The villagers cheered and began to run faster. Gameknight stood and waited as they passed, so he could bring up the rear. He wanted to make sure no one was left behind. At his side, he found Weaver, the boy's bright blue eyes almost glowing in the dim lunar lighting. Wilbur was walking along at his side.

"Let's go, Smithy," Weaver said as he moved next to one of the wounded soldiers and offered him assistance.

Gameknight turned and scanned the desert, looking for any unwelcome red fireflies. Fortunately, all he saw was empty sand and the occasional green, prickly cactus standing guard over the empty landscape. The silvery light from the half-filled moon was enough to see out a couple dozen blocks in all directions; they were alone.

"Oink, oink!" Wilbur insisted.

"I know, boy," Gameknight said. "We're going."

He patted the pig on the head, then turned and headed for the village. When he reached the last couple soldiers, he put his arm around a wood-carver that was limping badly to offer his support.

As he neared the desert community, Gameknight saw there were no defenses at all. The village was completely open on all sides. There was no watch-tower, no archer towers . . . not even holes in the ground to trap some monsters; the place was completely defenseless. They'd have to do something about that soon.

About twelve to fifteen homes and buildings made up the village, with the only source of water, a well, positioned at the center. Around the well, the newcomers were congregating, while some of the more severely wounded were already being taken into homes for treatment.

"Who is the leader of this village?" the User-that-is-not-a-user asked.

"I am," a tall, skinny NPC said. "Who is asking?"

Gameknight stepped forward and gazed at the village leader. He wore a dark brown smock with a light brown stripe running down the center. Neatly-combed long, gray hair fell down to his shoulders and across his back. From his clothing, Gameknight could tell this NPC was a farmer.

"I am . . . um, I'm Smithy, and I lead this army," Gameknight said.

"That's Smithy of the Two-Swords you're talking to!" one of the NPCs shouted.

The other warriors all shouted at the same time, "SMITHY!"

Gameknight raised his hands to calm the troops. He then turned and faced the villager.

"We are in need of assistance, Farmer," Gameknight said. "We're embroiled in a war and need supplies."

"A war? We don't want any part of a war," Farmer said warily.

"It's too late," Weaver snapped. "You're involved whether you know it or not."

"Weaver, please. Be quiet and let me handle this," Gameknight said.

"What is the boy talking about?" Farmer asked.

"Well . . ." Gameknight explained Herobrine and the monster army that they'd defeated. He also explained Herobrine's desire to destroy all the villagers across Minecraft. "You see, Herobrine wants the Overworld for the monsters. He will destroy every villager just out of spite."

Farmer did not reply; he just stood there, considering the information. He glanced around at his own villagers, their concerned eyes focused on him. But then one of them nodded their blocky heads, then another, and then another.

Gameknight smiled.

"Then we must help," Farmer said. "We will do as you ask, Smithy. Just tell us what you need."

"Excellent," Gameknight said. "First, we need help with our wounded."

"The most severe have already been taken into our homes," Farmer said. "What else?"

"We need to get a wall built around this village as quickly as possible," Gameknight explained. "As soon as Herobrine figures out we're here, he'll throw everything he has at us."

Farmer pointed at a group of builders and nodded. Instantly they began to work, placing a line of cobblestone around the homes and buildings, marking the location of the fortifications.

"Next, we need a watchtower so we can see the monsters when they're approaching."

Farmer gestured to another set of villagers. They were masons and knew exactly what to do. With cobblestone in hand, they ran to the center of the village and began outlining where the tower would stand.

"And lastly, we'll need a lot of stone and a crafting chamber," Gameknight said. "Diggers, get to work. You know what to do."

The stocky NPCs moved to the corner of the outlined watchtower and began to carve steps into the ground, constructing a secret tunnel that would lead to the crafting chamber that didn't exist. Not yet, at least.

"You act like you've done this before," Farmer said as they watched.

"Sadly, I've done this a lot in the past." *Or, in the future, rather*, Gameknight thought. "We also need food."

"You are welcome to the crops we have in the fields, but sadly, that will likely not be enough for everyone," Farmer said.

"Then we'll expand the fields and grow more wheat and melons. But we need food now; we're almost out," Gameknight said. "Farmer, where do you go if you need to hunt?"

"There is a birch forest not too far away, but you'll never find it at night," the village leader said. "To get to it, you must get across the Great Chasm that lies to the east. It runs through many biomes and can only be crossed at one place: the Midnight Bridge. On the other side of the bridge, you'll find a forest biome rich with cows and chickens and pigs," Farmer said.

Wilbur oinked and moved behind Gameknight.

"Don't worry, you'll be safe here," he said to the pig, then raised his voice so all could hear him. "We must keep our pig mascot safe. Smithy would be very, very disappointed if someone thought this pig might make a good snack . . . right?"

"SMITHY!" the villagers replied in agreement.

Gameknight smiled and patted Wilbur on the head.

"I'll keep an eye on your friend while you're away," Farmer said, turning to the animal. "I have a little girl that would love to meet you."

"Oink," Wilbur replied happily.

"Excellent," Gameknight said.

"Smithy . . . I wanna go," Weaver said.

Gameknight turned and could see the boy was eager to leave and help the army.

"I'm good with a bow," he added, "and can climb any tree to get apples."

"OK, Weaver, you and I will—" Gameknight started to say but was interrupted.

"And I'm going wherever Smithy goes," Fencer said, then folded his arms across his chest, daring anyone to challenge him.

Gameknight flashed his newfound friend a smile, then glanced at Farmer. "Can you give us a guide so that we can find this bridge and gather some food?"

The NPC scanned the village for someone not yet busy. Gameknight could see a stocky NPC leaning against a building with an axe in his hands. He wore a charcoal-gray smock with a brown stripe running down the center. His axe seemed razor-sharp, as if it had seen little use, even though the villager handled it as if he were an expert. Standing there, gazing out into the darkness, it seemed like he had nothing to do.

"What about him?" Gameknight asked, pointing at the NPC.

"Well . . ." Farmer said.

The village leader looked around for someone else, but all the other villagers were busy with building or digging or tending to the wounded.

"OK. He doesn't do anything useful around here anyway. We can spare him," Farmer said reluctantly. "Carver can be your guide."

The stocky NPC stood up straight and held his axe in his right hand.

"Take them to the forest," Farmer said, an angry tone in his voice.

The village leader then turned and left the group to take Wilbur toward his home.

Gameknight glanced at Carver. The NPC looked back with bright green eyes filled with an emptiness the User-that-is-not-a-user instantly recognized. It was the look of someone that did not belong, something that Gameknight had felt many times . . . being an outsider. The User-that-is-not-a-user had felt that at school all the time, having lunch alone, spending time in the library alone . . . few understood him there. When he'd been transported into Minecraft and found that he'd traveled into the past, that was originally how Smithy's village made him feel: like an outsider.

But now, in the guise of Smithy, he had been accepted, and it felt great, even though it was not terribly sincere. Gameknight was afraid to remove his helmet and show everyone who he really was. Living a lie was not a very good idea, but right now, the village needed a strong leader, and that leader was Smithy. If he exposed his secret now, it could make their army fall apart, and then they certainly would no longer accept him.

Gameknight wasn't sure why Carver felt so alone, but he could certainly sympathize with him.

"Come on," Carver said simply. "Let's get moving."

The NPC trudged off to the east, with Fencer, Weaver, and Gameknight following close behind.

# CHAPTER 5
# HUNTING

Carver led them to the southeast, shifting from walking to running periodically to move as quickly as possible. Rather than heading in a straight path, the NPC took a circuitous path through the empty landscape, curving his way around hills and dunes. It made the trek a little easier, and also kept them hidden from any unwanted eyes.

An uneasy quiet seemed to wrap itself around the four companions. Perhaps it was the impending threat of Herobrine, or maybe it was Carver's reluctance to go with them. In either case, no one dared violate the troubled silence. No one spoke, nor needed to; they were only required to follow their guide and find food when they reached the forest.

Glancing overhead, the User-that-is-not-a-user stared up at the stars sparkling down upon him. It always made him wonder what was out there . . . other planets, other dimensions? Or were the stars just decorations pasted on the ceiling of Minecraft to add a bit of mystery? Gameknight always wondered about that, but never had the time to really do any investigating.

Suddenly, some of the stars disappeared. Surveying the sky, he could see groups of clouds moving overhead, blotting out the heavenly canopy. Thicker clouds were now visible in the distance, with a solid grayish-white layer approaching from the east. Right now, the half-filled moon was still shining down upon them, but Gameknight could see it would soon succumb to a blanket of clouds and be blocked from view.

*Crunch!*

The noise seemed magnified by the silence of the desert.

Gameknight looked down and found he'd stepped on one of the small dried bushes that dotted the arid landscape. Pulling his leather boot out of the dry remains, the bush crunched again loudly. Standing perfectly still, he listened for any monsters that might have heard the sound. Fortunately, none seemed near.

Breathing a sigh of relief, Gameknight continued following the footsteps of the others.

"Maybe you should watch where you're walking," Fencer suggested with a smile.

"Big help, thanks," Gameknight replied, rolling his eyes.

They continued their journey, following close behind the stoic Carver. The gloom deepened as clouds drifted across overhead and blocked out the moon completely. With the stars and moon gone, the sky was now pitch black. Then, it started to rain, giving the four companions a brief respite from the blistering heat of the desert but soaking them to the bone.

"We're almost there," Carver said quietly as he wiped moisture from his flat forehead. "From here on, we go south." He glanced at Gameknight999. "Keep your eyes on the ground, so none of you fall to your deaths."

"Good advice," Fencer said.

Carver scowled at the sarcastic remark.

"The Great Chasm is right next to us," Carver continued. "In this darkness, you can't see it, but if you approach slowly, you'll see the edge and hopefully you won't fall in."

Gameknight moved cautiously to the edge and peered down. A jagged gash was carved into the landscape, and only the orange glow of the lava spilling across the distant floor below revealed its presence. It was nearly impossible to see, the darkness of the landscape merging into the nearly vertical walls of the Chasm. From this height, those who fell into it would certainly plummet to their deaths.

Faint moans floated up out of the ravine, along with the occasional clattering of bones. The User-that-is-not-a-user was certain there were monsters down there, but in the gloomy light, it was difficult to see any details. Only when the monsters veered close to the lava were they visible.

"Come on," Carver said. "The bridge is this way."

They followed Carver as he moved along the edge of the precipice. Their boots shuffled across the sandy ground, making a raspy sound that filled the air. Eventually, Gameknight began to notice the sounds of monsters trickling out of the Great Chasm, growing slightly louder. The sounds made the tiny hairs on the back of his square neck stand up on end. But as long as the monster sounds were so faint, the User-that-is-not-a-user knew they were far away. That's what he kept telling himself, anyway.

"Here it is," Carver said after a long while, as he slowed.

"Where?" Gameknight asked.

Carver smiled at the others, then stepped up to the edge of the Chasm and sprinted forward half-a-dozen blocks.

"Carver, look out!" Weaver exclaimed.

But the big NPC just stood there over the Chasm as if he were floating in mid-air. Reaching into his inventory, the NPC pulled out a torch and held it high over his head. It sputtered and sizzled in the rain but kept burning, casting a flickering circle of light that bathed the area around him in a warm yellow glow. A dark flat sheet of something sat under his feet. Tiny purple crystals sparkled in the torchlight like rare gems embedded within the blocks that made up the structure. They gave it an almost magical appearance.

"It's a bridge!" Weaver exclaimed.

"An obsidian bridge," Fencer said with amazement.

Gameknight said nothing. He just surveyed the object, noting the design and construction. When Carver put the torch away, Gameknight could still see it, for now he knew what to look for.

It was a classic bridge structure with a long, flat pathway that stretched from one side of the Chasm to the other. Tall vertical supports reached from the floor of the steep ravine all the way up to the bridge, then continued another dozen blocks upward above the path. From the top of those vertical supports, Gameknight could see obsidian blocks positioned in such a way that they formed a wide, sweeping arc, like you'd see on a bridge in the physical world. The arcs swooped high overhead, stretching from support to support, giving the impression that they somehow were helping to hold up the span of the bridge. Between the vertical supports that plunged down into the chasm, there were crisscrossing structures connecting the pair of columns, likely intended to keep the bridge from swaying in high winds.

It seemed like the designer of this bridge wanted to avoid the same bad result of the Tacoma Narrows Bridge in the real world . . . which was curious. Clearly, someone who had seen a bridge in the physical world, and not an NPC, had built this bridge. It looked a lot like the Golden Gate Bridge in San Francisco.

The fact of the matter was that none of the supports were necessary. The builder could have just extended a line of obsidian straight across the gorge, ignoring any of the cross members or arcing supports. Because of the strange rules of physics in Minecraft, the extra reinforcements were not necessary, so here they were only cosmetic. *This is very strange indeed,* Gameknight thought.

Stepping cautiously onto the bridge, the party followed Carver as he continued to lead the way to their destination. Below, Gameknight could see the orange glow of lava lighting the bottom. From directly in the center, he could see monsters moving about, but there were not as many as he had expected . . . and for some reason, that worried him.

When they reached the opposite end of the Bridge, the desert gave way to a thick birch forest.

At the same time, the clouds drifted away from the moon, allowing its silvery light to shine down on the terrain. The white-barked trees almost glowed in the lunar illumination, inviting the four travelers into their leafy embrace.

"OK, let's look for food," Gameknight said. "We should be able to find chickens and cows. Any grass you see, dig it up. We can use the seeds to grow some wheat as well."

The group moved quickly through the forest. Gameknight and Weaver focused on collecting grass seeds and apples, while Carver and Fencer collected the beef and chicken. After fifteen minutes of foraging, Gameknight noticed that the sounds of the forest had changed. The soft moans that trickled out of the Great Chasm were suddenly joined by more voices, new growls that were much louder . . . and *much* closer.

"Zombies . . ." Carver said as he drew his iron sword.

Gameknight stopped and glanced around. The dark forest made it difficult to see anything. Reaching into his inventory, he pulled out a torch and placed it on the ground.

"This way," the User-that-is-not-a-user said. "Everyone, stay close together."

Suddenly, more sad moans came from behind them; there was another group of monsters on the other side.

"They're trying to surround us!" Fencer said.

He pulled out his bow and fired toward the sound. The arrow whizzed through the air and disappeared into the darkness.

"Wait until you can see what you're shooting at," Gameknight chided.

Planting another torch on the ground, he led them away from the groaning monsters. *Grrrrrr . . .* Another group filled the night with their angry voices, this one directly before them. Placing another torch into the ground, Gameknight drew his two iron swords. Now the growling came from all sides. His heart pounded in his chest like a mighty tribal drum and his breathing quickened. Cubes of sweat trickled down his forehead, finding their way into his eyes. It stung. The sounds of the monsters, mixed with his imagination, made it seem like there were a hundred zombies out there in the shadows.

"What do we do?" Weaver asked nervously.

Gameknight didn't reply, for there was nothing he could think of to say that would make the situation better.

*I was their leader, and look what I've gotten them into*, Gameknight thought.

"Here's what we'll do," Gameknight said. "As soon as—"

He stopped short when the monsters suddenly emerged from the darkness. Glistening, razor-sharp claws reflected the flickering light from the torch, making them appear even more terrifying.

"We're surrounded!" Carver exclaimed.

"Quick, everyone get back-to-back, facing outward," Gameknight said.

"What do we do? What do we do?" Weaver said, fear in his voice. "Smithy, what are we gonna do?!"

Gameknight didn't answer. He knew they could do only one thing . . . wait, and then fight.

# CHAPTER 6

# ZOMBIE BATTLE

The monsters saw Gameknight's dual swords and they hesitated for just a moment; that was a mistake. The User-that-is-not-a-user leapt forward and slashed at one of the monsters before it even knew what was happening. He struck it three times, causing it to flash red, then disappear with a *pop!* leaving behind a piece of zombie flesh and three glowing balls of experience points (XP). The other monsters growled in anger, then lunged at him.

Expecting this reaction, Gameknight moved back again so that he was back-to-back with his friends.

"What were you thinking?" Fencer asked. "'Maybe I'll just go out there and attack one of them, to see if they'll go away?'"

"I don't know," Gameknight replied. "I guess sometimes it's better to not think and just do."

*Grrrroar!* The zombies growled and moaned, then shuffled forward, their claws outstretched.

"Remember, watch the people around you and try to protect them while they protect you,"

Gameknight said. "If we work together, then this won't be too difficult."

"Yeah," Weaver agreed. "After all, there's only twelve of them now. That means we just need to take care of three zombies each and it's over."

"Thanks for the math lesson, Professor," Fencer said with a grin.

The monsters charged forward, claws slashing through the air. Gameknight blocked one set of razor-sharp nails with his right sword as another set headed straight for Carver. He reached out with his left blade and blocked the creature. But because he shifted his attention away, the first monster was now able to swipe at his shoulder. Zombie claws scratched deep into his leather armor. It made a sick, scratching sound, like a dull saw cutting wood. Fortunately, the pointed nails did not penetrate through to the soft flesh that lay underneath. Swinging one of his swords with all his strength, he brought it down on the monster, smashing its arm and making it flash red.

"Grrr," Weaver grunted as a monster scored a hit on the young NPC.

"I'll come help, Weaver," Gameknight shouted.

"Stay where you are, Smithy, we got this," Fencer said in between attacks.

Gameknight stayed put and focused on the monsters before him. His swords became a blur and he slashed at a zombie. A fist of claws came at his head. He ducked under the attack, then struck the monster's chest. It flashed red for the last time, then disappeared. Without pause, he lunged at the creature that was attacking Carver. The NPC was swinging his iron sword at the monsters, but Gameknight could tell he was not very comfortable with the weapon—or very good.

Slashing with his right blade, he struck at a zombie's ribs, making it take damage, then brought his other blade down upon it as the monster turned to face him. He did this again with the creature to his left, poking then swinging an overhead attack.

"Carver, Fencer: hit them when they turn to face me," Gameknight said.

He didn't wait for a reply—he just jabbed at the monsters again. When the tip of his sword found soft zombie flesh, the creatures turned to attack him. That was when Fencer and Carver knew to attack. Feeling the bite of their blades, the monsters turned back to their attackers, leaving Gameknight open to bring down his deadly swords. With the defenders working together, and the zombies working only as individuals, the monsters didn't last very long. They quickly began to fall, each one with a confused and terrified look on its decaying, scarred face.

Finally, only two remained. One of the zombies, probably the leader, had never moved forward to join in the fighting. Instead, he'd stood just on the edge of the light cast by the torch, watching and growling at his comrades. The other now stood bravely alone before the four villagers, unwilling to yield.

"You are defeated, both of you," Gameknight shouted.

The monster in front growled and snarled while the leader turned and fled into the darkness.

"Should we go after him?" Weaver asked.

"Not in this dark forest," Carver said. "Who knows how many of them are still out there?"

"Carver is right," Gameknight added. "Besides, we have one here that should have some very interesting information to tell us."

The zombie glared at the villagers, then moaned a sorrowful moan.

Gameknight pointed his two swords at the creature's neck, then moved until the points were just barely touching its decaying skin.

"If you wish to live, then you'll answer some questions," the User-that-is-not-a-user said. "If we're satisfied with your answers, then we will let you join your friend that abandoned you. But if you refuse to answer our questions, then you'll join those that fell in battle. Now, are you going to cooperate?"

"Grrr . . . this zombie will say nothing," the monster growled.

"I figured as much," Gameknight said.

He jabbed at the creature with his sword, causing it to flash red as it took damage to its HP.

"You will only withstand two more of those before your HP is gone and you disappear," Gameknight said. "Now, I'll ask you again: Are you going to cooperate?"

"Let's just destroy him and get out of here," Fencer said impatiently.

"Now hold on, Fencer," Gameknight said. "I think our zombie friend is going to be reasonable. I'm pretty sure he doesn't want to disappear forever: Do you?"

The zombie growled.

"Tell us where Herobrine is hiding and what he's up to," Gameknight demanded.

The monster swiped at him with its pointy claws. The User-that-is-not-a-user stepped back, letting the razor-sharp nails flash past his face, making the faintest whistling sound as they cut through the air.

Gameknight hit him with his sword, causing the zombie to flash red again. The monster yelled out in pain as its HP dropped dangerously low, then fell to its knees, its strength waning.

"This is your last chance," the User-that-is-not-a-user warned. "The next time I hit you will be the last. Tell me what I want to know."

"Fine. This zombie will speak," the monster rasped, its breathing strained.

"Where are Herobrine and his army?" Fencer asked.

The monster glared up at the NPC and snarled.

"Herobrine is hiding at Dragon's Teeth," the zombie said reluctantly. "The Maker is amassing a huge army that will destroy all the villagers. This time, there will be so many monsters that the blacksmith's forces won't stand a chance. This zombie looks forward to seeing Smithy perish."

"How dare you!" Weaver yelled, and raised his sword for a final, fatal blow.

"No," Gameknight said. "Lower your sword, Weaver."

"But he said—"

"I said no," he insisted. "I promised that we would free this zombie if he answered our questions. Now it is time to let him go. Everyone step back."

Gameknight moved backward, then glared at his companions until they also moved away from the monster.

"Let it be known that Smithy keeps his word," Gameknight said. "Now, be gone from here. Maybe your friend is out there in the darkness is waiting for you."

"Not likely," the zombie growled as it struggled to stand. The creature glared at Gameknight one more time, then turned and disappeared into the night.

"I think we should get back and tell the others what we've learned," Fencer said.

"I agree," Gameknight said, then faced Carver. "Do you know where this place, Dragon's Teeth, is located?"

Carver nodded his head.

"Good," he replied. "We might need to take a little trip there soon."

"You're thinking maybe we should go to where Herobrine is building up his army?" Fencer asked.

Gameknight nodded his square head.

"You *are* crazy," his friend said.

"Perhaps," the User-that-is-not-a-user replied. "But knowledge is power, and right now, I feel powerless."

"Come on, the bridge is this way," Carver said and he led them back toward their desert village.

# CHAPTER 7

# SHADOW-CRAFTERS

A sparkling purple mist formed right in front of Herobrine, clouding his view of the four mighty stone spires that climbed upward into the sky. He took a step back and waited, knowing what would be filling the cloud. Suddenly, a dark red Enderman appeared amid the lavender particles.

"Erebus, what have you to report?" Herobrine asked.

"As you predicted, more Endermen are spawning in the obsidian cave," Erebus said. "Soon, there will be many of my brothers and sisters ready to attack the villagers."

Nearby, more clouds of purple mist formed, filled with the tall, lanky creatures. Their black skin stood out against the gray stone that made up Dragon's Teeth.

Herobrine glanced at the newly-arrived monsters, then looked up at the four peaks that stood tall and majestic around him. The mountains were spread out as if on the corners of a square, each one jutting straight up into the air like a gigantic monster's tooth. The sides of the mountains were incredibly steep and impossible to climb. Made completely of stone, the four rocky spikes stood above the level of the clouds, making their summits difficult to see. One of the mountains had lava spilling down the side, casting a warm orange glow on the surroundings. Groups of blazes bathed in the liquid stone, the intense heat replenishing their HP and making the internal flame that formed their bodies burn with delight. Even with the moon covered by dark rain clouds, the lava provided enough light for Herobrine to see clearly.

Opposite the lava fall was another "tooth" which boasted a waterfall. The flowing liquid spilled down the steep side, then struck a stone block and divided into two separate rivers. One of them streamed down the mountain until it crashed into the lava, forming a wide slab of sparkling purple blocks. The obsidian reflected the light from the lava in all directions.

At the center of Dragon's Teeth was a wide hole that was roughly shaped like the yawning mouth of some kind of massive primordial beast. Blocks of stone jutted out from the edge, making it look as if it were lined with deadly teeth. Down the throat of the monstrous opening was a tunnel that plunged down into the ground. The passage was dark and steep and ended abruptly after bending into a horizontal cave. Soon, Herobrine would remake that chamber into something much bigger, but not now.

Glancing back at the newly arrived Endermen, Herobrine watched as they stepped into the flowing water and bathed. Apparently, the Maker had accidently given the creatures the smallest piece of his own vanity. Herobrine always wanted to look immaculate and clean so that his visage could frighten his victims. This desire to stay clean had been accidently transferred to the Endermen. Now, to replenish their HP, the dark monsters had to stand in a pool of water and bathe themselves. It was their greatest joy, to become clean, and it fed their HP; it was a double bonus for them, though it frustrated Herobrine a bit.

Just then, a zombie approached, staggering around the boiling pool of molten stone.

"Maker . . . Maker!" the creature yelled.

Herobrine turned toward the creature, then teleported to the struggling monster.

"What are you moaning about?" Herobrine asked.

"The enemy . . . the blacksmith . . . has been seen," the zombie stammered, his HP slowly failing.

"You saw him?"

The zombie nodded its scarred head. "The squad of zombies came across the blacksmith in the birch forest," he reported.

"Did you kill him?" Herobrine asked. "I hope you made him suffer first."

The zombie glanced down at the ground, clearly ashamed.

"The blacksmith and three NPCs destroyed a dozen zombies," the squad leader said. "Only this zombie escaped."

"There were twelve of you and only four of them," Herobrine said, "and you LOST?!"

His eyes glowed bright as rage boiled over within his soul. Drawing his sword, he slashed at the monster, destroying it with a single hit. He gazed around and saw that many of the monsters had seen him destroy the zombie. Good!

"I need stronger monsters," Herobrine said aloud to himself. "These creatures that Minecraft has given me are pathetic and useless."

He clasped his hands behind his back and paced back and forth, considering what to do. Suddenly, Erebus materialized two blocks away. Herobrine noticed the king of the Endermen was wise and always stayed out of arm's reach when the Maker was angry (which was frequent these days).

"I need stronger monsters," Herobrine growled again.

"Perhaps you can remake them as you did when you created the Endermen," Erebus said.

"I can't waste my time trying to improve the zombies, because then I'll need to do it with the skeletons and the spiders and the creepers. Too much work for someone as important as me."

"Perhaps you need to create some crafters to do the task for you," the king of the Endermen suggested.

"What did you say?" Herobrine asked.

Erebus cast a nervous gaze toward his Maker, then took a step back.

"Of course," Herobrine mused, his mind racing. "I need to create my own shadow-crafters."

Closing his eyes, he gathered his viral artificial intelligence powers. Slowly, his hands began to glow a sickly pale yellow as the power grew; Herobrine loved it. Gradually, the glow oozed up his arms until it reached his shoulders. With his hands balled into fists, he knelt and plunged them into the stone floor of Dragon's Teeth. The ground seemed to shake with fear as he drove his arms deeper and deeper into the rocky blocks.

With his arms elbow-deep into the ground, he drove his awareness into the mechanism of Minecraft. Slowly he drew together strands of code, merging them together with the essence of various monsters, combining the two in an effort to create something new. He closed his eyes and concentrated, using every bit of code-altering skill the virus possessed, until he'd finished the first of them. Herobrine could sense one of his new creations coming into existence before him, but he did not bother to open his eyes and look; he still had many more to make.

He created more and more of the creatures, giving each just the smallest bit of his code-altering capabilities, but still reserving the vast storehouse of power for himself so that none of these creatures could ever consider taking over. Merging each creation with a different monster or aspect of Minecraft, Herobrine created his new army.

When he was finished, he withdrew his arms from the surface of Minecraft and opened his eyes. Before him stood a vast array of creatures, each similar to an NPC, but each also drastically different. The nearest had putrid-looking green skin, its arms and face covered in scars. The creature was completely bald and wore a light blue tattered shirt, its dark blue pants torn in many places. Instantly, Herobrine knew who it was.

"Ahh . . . Zombiebrine," Herobrine said as he gestured to the creature. "You have much to do."

He then addressed many of the others.

"Creeperbrine, Skeletonbrine, Spiderbrine . . . you *all* have much to do," Herobrine said, an eerie, malicious smile on his square face. Around him stood many of the new creatures, each different in appearance and purpose. "You are my shadow-crafters, my special creations that will make the monster army stronger, more powerful, and more vicious. With your help, we will craft a fighting force that will sweep across the land and destroy every villager. With your help, everything that is bad for the NPCs will become worse. Lava will be hotter, caves darker, and arrows sharper. We will enter a new era of monsters, with the Overworld soon cleansed of that infestation known as villagers."

The shadow-crafters each growled and clapped and bubbled and clattered as befitting their specialty. It made Herobrine smile.

"All of you, get to work, right away," Herobrine instructed. "There is a cave underground where you can work . . . now go!"

The army of shadow-crafters turned and headed toward the gaping hole that sat at the center of Dragon's Teeth.

"Erebus, where are you?" Herobrine yelled.

The king of the Endermen materialized directly in front of his Maker.

"I am here," Erebus said.

"I have a task for you," Herobrine said with a devious smile.

"Are we to attack the blacksmith and his forces?" the Endermen king asked.

"We aren't ready yet, but soon. For now, let the NPCs contemplate their doom. The fear that is gathering within each one of them will do more to unravel their courage than your fists could." Herobrine's eyes then glowed bright with evil thought. "Find the blacksmith and his followers, then report their position to me. After that, send one of your Endermen every so often close to them, for the sole purpose of screeching awfully into the night. Remind them that you are there, but do not attack and make sure you are not seen. An enemy that is not visible will seem more terrifying in their imaginations. Ha ha ha ha . . ."

Erebus's eyes glowed white with glee at the thought of the villagers cowering in the darkness. *What idiots!* he thought.

"When we can feel their fear growing, then we will attack," Herobrine explained. "Be sure not to harm the blacksmith. I want him alive so that he can watch the suffering of his friends."

Erebus smiled a vile, malicious smile, his red eyes glowing like two brilliant lasers.

"Oh, and give the blacksmith a message," Herobrine said, whispering into the dark creature's ear.

Erebus cackled a spine-cringing laugh, then disappeared in a cloud of purple mist, his laugh echoing off Dragon's Teeth, making Minecraft itself shudder in fear.

# CHAPTER 8
# UNSEEN ENEMIES

The desert village appeared in the distance, just as the square, yellow face of the sun was emerging from behind the eastern horizon. Splashes of red and orange stained the dark overhead canopy, erasing the stars faintly peeking through the night sky.

"Something looks different," Carver said as he stared toward the desert community.

"What do you mean?" Fencer asked.

"I don't know," the stocky NPC replied. "I can't put my finger on it."

"You think the village was attacked?" Weaver asked.

Carver didn't answer; he just looked straight ahead at his home as they made their way over the sand dune before them. Gameknight could feel the tension in the NPC and knew he was scared something might have happened to his friends and family.

Reaching into his inventory, Carver pulled out his axe and began to pass it nervously from hand to hand. The razor-sharp tool seemed to ease his fears a little.

They crested the sand dune and ran down the other side. In the brightening light, the village was easier to see. A huge new cobblestone wall stood before them. Though it was not complete yet, it was beautiful to see. Workers moved all across the fortification like an army of tiny ants, walking along the top and placing blocks while, at the same time, watching the landscape for threats.

"Walls . . . nice," Gameknight said with a grin. "That'll make it harder for Herobrine to attack. But it won't stop him. We still have much to do."

A strange sound, like the combination of a cat's yowl and a baby's cry, trickled down from above. Instantly, Gameknight drew his bow and ducked, searching for some place to hide.

"Everyone get to cover!" Gameknight shouted.

Carver, Fencer, and Weaver just stopped and stared at the user in the blacksmith's garb.

"What are you doing?" Fencer asked.

"Ghasts," Gameknight snapped. "I heard ghasts."

"What are 'ghasts'?" Weaver asked, confused.

Casting a glance skyward, Gameknight saw large white cubes floating amongst the clouds. Nine long tentacles hung below each creature, dragging through the clouds like fingers through a pool of calm water. Huge, baby-like faces adorned each cube, their big eyes gazing down at the trio.

"Those are ghasts," Gameknight said, pointing with his bow. "At least, they look a lot like ghasts . . ."

"Those things? They're harmless," Fencer said. "Everyone knows that, including you, Smithy," he added, giving him a quick, frustrated look.

"Umm . . . yeah, of course," Gameknight replied. "It's just that I heard some of them attacked a village far away, shooting fireballs at them."

"Fireballs?" Weaver said incredulously, looking up at the sky. "Those things?"

"Why would they attack a village?" Carver asked. "They're part of the clouds. They just fly around up there, just pure white decorations in the sky."

As one moved a little lower, Gameknight could see that the huge boxy creatures were completely devoid of markings on their skin. No dark scars marked their face or bodies, and there were no tear-like markings under their eyes, like the ghasts he was familiar with. They were as pure as the boxy clouds in which they played.

*Maybe ghasts aren't dangerous in this time?* Gameknight thought. *I wonder what changes to make them so dangerous in the future.*

"You're right. I don't know what I was thinking," Gameknight said as he put away his bow. He cast an apologetic glance to Fencer, then stared up at the creatures in the sky nervously.

*This is weird,* he thought, then turned away and continued heading for the desert village.

"PEOPLE APPROACHING FROM THE EAST!" a voice shouted from the top of the fortified wall.

Instantly, the battlements filled with archers and swordsmen, and the east wall bristled with soldiers. Gameknight felt a sense of pride at their fast response. The desert community was obviously taking security very seriously.

When they recognized the party, the village gates were opened, and the four comrades walked in, the wooden doors closing immediately after they'd entered. Glancing around, Gameknight could see the village had been expanded. The area for crops had been significantly enlarged, with the available dirt already placed, tilled, and planted. Pulling the dirt and seeds he'd collected in the forest out of his inventory, he gave them to one of the farmers. The chicken and beef that had been collected was distributed among the hungriest, and the rest was cooked and stored in the village's storeroom.

At the center of the village, a tall watchtower rose high into the air. Workers were placing cobblestone blocks at the top, building it up skyward, while others completed the floors inside. One of the NPCs finished a wall, then moved to the north edge of the tower and jumped off. Gameknight gasped as he fell, but the worker knew what he was doing. He landed with a splash in a shallow pool of water; it was an easy and efficient way to get down.

Farmer approached the party.

"You found food and seed," the old village leader said.

"Yes," Gameknight replied. "Carver knew right where to take us."

"Hmm . . . I guess he did well," Farmer added. "Maybe he should be a hunter."

"I'm a carver, and you know it," Carver snapped, then spun around and stormed off.

"What was that about?" Fencer asked as he moved closer.

"Well, you see, Carver has had a difficult time finding his place in the village," Farmer said. "But that's not important right now. What do you think of the improvements to the village?"

"They are fantastic," Gameknight said. "The wall is excellent, and the watchtower is coming along nicely. Are you building the crafting chamber?"

"Where do you think all the cobblestone came from?" Farmer asked.

Gameknight nodded his head and smiled.

"Smithy, tell him what we learned," Fencer said.

The smile on Gameknight's square face faded to a scowl.

"What?" Farmer asked.

"We know Herobrine is gathering another monster army," Gameknight said.

"Where did you hear that?" Farmer asked.

"We captured a zombie and made him talk," Weaver added excitedly.

Gameknight reached out and tussled the boy's hair. "Weaver is right. We were able to get some information out of a zombie," the User-that-is-not-a-user explained. "Herobrine is gathering at something called Dragon's Teeth. Does that mean anything to you?"

"Yes," Farmer replied. "It is on the other side of the Great Chasm. It can be reached by going across Midnight Bridge from the south, or by going up and around the end of the Great Chasm from the north. It's in an extreme hills biome."

"That will mean a lot of tunnels and caverns," Gameknight said. "He'll likely have the king of the creepers and the spider queen with him. We can expect a lot of those creatures soon, but I'm sure that evil virus has more in store for us." He turned and faced Farmer. "We're going to need a lot more villagers, I fear, very soon."

Suddenly, a strange screeching sound floated out of the desert. It was barely audible over the activity of the busy village. Tiny square goose bumps formed on the back of Gameknight's arms.

"Did you hear that?" the User-that-is-not-a-user asked.

"What are you talking about?" Fencer asked.

Another quiet, high-pitched screech reached Gameknight's ears. This time, he could tell it was coming from the west.

"There it is again," he said. "It's coming from the west."

Drawing his sword, he ran to the stairs that led to the top of the fortified wall. Weaving around NPCs, he sprinted across the battlements until he was on the western wall. He stared out into the desert.

"Game . . . uhhh . . . I mean, Smithy, what are you doing?" Fencer asked as he caught up with him.

"I heard something," Gameknight said. "It was a noise I haven't heard for a long time, and I can't quite recognize it."

The screech was heard again, but this time it came from the south. It made the hairs on the back of Gameknight's neck stand up straight as a shiver went down his spine.

"You must have heard it that time," the User-that-is-not-a-user said.

Fencer nodded his head. "I've never heard any-thing like that before."

"I have . . . I just can't remember from where."

Gameknight glanced down and could see other villagers facing south, curious about the noise.

Just then, piercing screeches came out of the desert from the north and south, both at the same time. They were much louder this time, as if the source was either closer, or there were a lot of them. Whichever it was, Gameknight didn't like it.

"Everyone, get to your positions!" he shouted.

Someone started to bang a sword against an empty bucket, making a loud *CLANKING* sound. This caused everyone in the village to stop what they were doing and take their battle stations. Archers ran to the towers and walls while swordsmen stood near the village gates, ready to run out and attack.

The screeches sounded again, this time, from all sides. Some of the villagers were beginning to look afraid, the high-pitched wails chiseling away at their courage.

"I have to see what it is," Gameknight said.

He jumped from the wall and landed in a small pool of water that fed one of the wheat fields. Stepping out, he ran for the watchtower. Running through the entrance, he raced up the ladder that led to the higher levels. When he reached the top, he found Weaver already there, his young eyes gazing out into the seemingly empty desert.

"You see anything?" Gameknight asked.

"No," the young NPC replied.

The screeching sounded again, but this time it was from all sides. And in that instant, Gameknight remembered where he'd heard that sound before.

"Endermen," the User-that-is-not-a-user hissed.

"What?" Weaver asked.

Fencer finally made it to the top of the tower and stood at Gameknight's side.

"That sound is coming from Endermen," Gameknight said.

Just then, a group of dark creatures materialized in a cloud of purple mist on the tall sand dune that stood in front of the village gates. They were all pitch-black as if the monsters were moving shadows walking across the brightly lit desert sands.

"What are they?" Fencer asked.

"I told you, they're Endermen," Gameknight replied.

"Ender-what?"

Suddenly, more of them appeared on the dune. There were maybe thirty of them, all screeching and cackling at the top of their voices. The villagers behind the cobblestone walls cupped their hands to their ears to try to block out the terrible, spine-cringing sound.

And then the creatures disappeared—only to reappear suddenly inside the village, one of them materializing right in front of a warrior near the village gates.

"No, don't hit the—" Gameknight began to shout, but it was already too late.

The NPC swung his sword at the dark nightmare and struck it in the arm. The Enderman's eyes glowed bright white as it screeched a loud, high-pitched screech, signaling that it was enraged. The battle had begun.

# CHAPTER 9
# ENDERMEN

The Endermen became streaks of purple and black lightning. They flashed across the village, pummeling NPCs with their fists, then teleporting away just as a sword or arrow came sailing toward them. Their screeches and cackles filled the air as if the whole event were just some kind of wild, out-of-control party to them.

One of the monsters appeared before Gameknight on the tower. He ducked as a dark fist streaked toward his head. The monster then zipped away harmlessly as his iron sword sliced at its long, skinny legs.

"We have to get down there," Gameknight said to Fencer and Weaver.

He moved to the ladder and slid to the ground, his two companions a step behind. When he reached the ground floor, Gameknight sprinted out into the courtyard. With both swords drawn, he stood out in the middle so that he was easy to see.

"Come on, Endermen," Gameknight said confidently. "Come meet Smithy's blades!"

One of the dark monsters appeared in front of him. The User-that-is-not-a-user rolled to the side, then slashed at the legs again. The monster disappeared in a cloud of purple; Gameknight had expected that. He swung his swords behind him just as the monster materialized . . . they were so predictable. His blades bit into the dark clammy skin, making the creature screech in agony. Before it could teleport again, Gameknight brought his sword down upon its shoulder. The wounded Enderman teleported away, screaming in pain.

Suddenly, Weaver was at his side.

"Stand back-to-back," Gameknight said to the young boy. "When you see the purple mist, swing at it, whether there's something there or not."

Weaver cocked his side in confusion but said nothing. He just moved behind him with his iron sword ready.

An Enderman appeared in front of Gameknight. His blade slashed at the monster. The creature disappeared, only to reappear behind him, in front of Weaver. But the boy's sword was already moving, slashing at the lavender cloud that had formed. The monster materialized right as the youth's iron sword dug into his side. Screeching in pain, the monster disappeared, then materialized to the left. Gameknight charged, swinging both swords at the monster's head. The blade in his right hand missed, but then the User-that-is-not-a-user spun and swung his left sword at the lavender cloud forming near Weaver. Another screech of pain filled the air as Gameknight's sword scored a critical hit, followed by Weaver's. The monster disappeared, leaving behind three balls of XP and a strange, blue, translucent sphere.

Just then, Gameknight noticed the cries of pain filling the village, as black fists pummeled the villagers with a fury. The dark creatures were doing significant damage to the NPCs.

"Weaver, we need to act fast before anyone is killed," Gameknight said.

Putting away his swords, the User-that-is-not-a-user pulled out a bucket and filled it with water. He then dipped two more into the nearby well, with Weaver doing the same.

"Come on," Gameknight said.

He ran for the gates. That was where the largest concentration of NPC warriors and Endermen were located. When he drew near, both of them poured a bucket of water on the ground. The blue liquid quickly spread across the ground, pushing the warriors back and coating the legs of the Endermen.

"Now watch," Gameknight said with a grin.

But quickly that grin turned to a scowl.

He expected the skin on the Endermen to sizzle and burn when it came in contact with the water. But instead, the dark monsters seemed to enjoy being in the water. In fact, the flowing liquid drew more Endermen near, as if they wanted to bathe themselves. The warriors all backed up to watch the strange display: monsters stopping to bathe in the middle of a battle.

"Archers . . . fire!" Gameknight shouted.

Arrows rained down upon the monsters. He expected the Endermen to teleport away, but they were so distracted with their bathing that they didn't even notice the projectiles until they hit. The creatures screeched out in pain, but still continued to clean themselves, as if the bath somehow repaired the damage done by the projectiles.

Suddenly, a lone Enderman appeared at the top of the watchtower. It screeched a long, loud wail that caused the other dark monsters to stop what they were doing and glance up at their squad leader. Then they all disappeared, teleporting away to a sand dune far from the village.

"Blacksmith, you think you can hide from Herobrine here in this village," the black nightmare boomed. "But you are mistaken."

"You tell Herobine that we aren't hiding," Gameknight roared. "He should feel free to stop by any time." He turned and faced the villagers, some of whom were struggling to stand. A few were badly wounded and were eating apples and loaves of bread to help themselves heal. "What is it you want here, Endermen?" Gameknight was careful to look aside and not straight at the monster.

"I have come to deliver a message from Herobrine."

"And did this message come with instructions to hurt some of the villagers?" Gameknight asked.

"Of course it did," the shadowy creature replied with a smile.

"Deliver your message and be gone," the User-that-is-not-a-user growled.

"This is a reminder that there are things to fear in Minecraft, and the Maker, Herobrine, is not done with you. Soon, he will return to wreak his vengeance upon the villagers of the Overworld. And when he has destroyed all of you puny creatures, then the Overworld will belong to monsters, as it should. But for now, quake in fear, for our return is imminent!"

The monster disappeared in a cloud of purple mist, only to reappear in the distance with the other Endermen. Gameknight ran to the top of the fortified wall and stared out at them. All of the creatures, from this distance, appeared identical, jet-black and terrifying, their purple eyes glowing bright. But then he caught a glimpse of one of the monsters standing much farther away, just barely visible in the distance. It was colored a dark, dark red, like the color of dried blood. *It can't be,* Gameknight thought. Then the image was gone; it was likely a mirage formed by his own fears . . . and nightmares.

"We will be back soon," the Enderman screeched, then they all vanished.

Fencer and Farmer climbed the steps and moved to Gameknight's side.

"How do we fight monsters that can teleport away from us?" Farmer asked.

"There are tricks I can teach you that will help," Gameknight said.

"You mean like the water?" Farmer asked. "That worked great!"

"No, it didn't work at all," the User-that-is-not-a-user replied. "I expected the water to burn them, but instead, they seemed to like it."

"Who cares?" Fencer pointed out. "The water made them stop fighting."

"I didn't expect the Endermen to appear," Gameknight said. He turned and faced Fencer. "Why didn't Herobrine use the Endermen when we battled the zombie king?"

Fencer shrugged.

"I don't like this, not at all," Gameknight said. "Herobrine is up to something, and I think we're gonna need a lot more villagers in order to stop him." He glanced at Farmer. "*A lot* more!"

Farmer nodded, his long, gray hair falling across his face.

Gameknight turned and stared out into the desert at the spot where the Endermen had been standing. He shuddered as he imagined a hundred of those monsters coming to the village. Likely that would be part of Herobrine's plan.

*How are we gonna defend ourselves next time,* Gameknight thought. *What would Smithy do?*

He tried to imagine being as strong and brave as the legendary leader, but all he felt was empty. Pretending to be Smithy was just a pathetic lie, and all it made Gameknight feel was scared.

# CHAPTER 10

# PREPARATIONS

"Smithy . . . Smithy!" Fencer shouted. "Are you there? Wake up!"

"Sorry, I was just thinking about what to do next," Gameknight lied. Really, he was imaging all the terrible things that could happen to all these villagers.

"Oink," Wilbur said as the animal rubbed against his leg.

The User-that-is-not-a-user suspected the creature could somehow sense his emotions, and that the little pig had felt Gameknight's fear. He reached down and patted the animal on the head.

"Well, you want to share with us what you have in mind?" Fencer said.

Looking up, he nodded, then moved to Fencer's side.

"First of all, we need to finish the defenses," Gameknight said.

"But how are we going to keep those monsters from attacking us . . . what did you call them?" Carver asked.

"They're called Endermen," Gameknight said, "and they *can* be stopped. You just need to know how to fight them." He looked up at the stocky NPC. "I can teach you all how to do it."

"Okay, what next?" Farmer asked.

"We need to finish the defenses around the village," Gameknight said. "If Herobrine sees the defenses are incomplete, he will attack before we're ready. I just hope the Enderman didn't notice."

"We'll put everyone to work finishing the defenses," Farmer said.

"That's good," Gameknight added, "but I've learned it can be a mistake to just wait for Herobrine to attack. Walls can only do so much, and we have a limited number of villagers with us."

"We can send out some runners to the neighboring villages," Carver said.

Farmer frowned at the villager for speaking up. Carver scowled right back at him.

"That would be helpful, but nobody should go anywhere alone," Gameknight said.

"Understood." Farmer turned and nodded to a group of villagers listening. "They'll all go in pairs and run to the villages nearby. Then we'll have runners head out from those villages. Soon, we'll have our own massive army to face off against Herobrine."

The runners disappeared into one of the blocky homes momentarily, then returned.

"We'll be back soon with help," one of the runners said. Then the group of villagers all ran out of the village and across the brightly lit desert, each protected with just a leather tunic so they could run as quickly as possible, a bow in their stubby hands.

"While we're waiting for them," Farmer said, "let's start building some walls."

"Weaver," Gameknight said. "Go help with the crafting chamber. When it is complete, we need to start on tunnels that go to the other villages for the—"

"For the minecart network," the young boy said with a smile.

Gameknight nodded.

"Carver, come help me outside the walls," Gameknight said.

"What are we going to do?" he asked.

"I'll show you."

Gameknight walked through the village gates, then began digging a tunnel under the sand, replacing the falling blocks with sandstone. Next to the tunnel, he put holes two blocks deep.

"Any monster that falls into these holes will be trapped," Gameknight said. "But villagers will be able to attack their legs from this tunnel. These are called 'murder holes,' and they will help if there is another attack."

The two of them worked in silence, carving through the desert terrain, building traps that would hopefully help save the lives of the villagers.

"What do you think Herobrine is going to do?" Carver asked.

"I think he will do what the Enderman said. He's going to make everyone suffer his wrath," Gameknight replied. "But I'm not gonna just sit here and wait for him to come. The only way to deal with a bully like Herobrine is to change the situation. We aren't going to just stand here and wait. I have another idea."

"What's that, Smithy?" Carver asked.

"Let's finish these traps, then discuss it with Farmer," Gameknight replied.

Carver scowled and seemed hurt, but turned and focused his anger instead on the sandstone before him. They finished the tunnel around the front of the village, then carved a passage that ran under the fortified wall, and dug an entrance to the subterranean network. When they climbed out, they found Farmer and Fencer discussing the village defenses near the central well.

"Smithy, we need to make a plan for what's next," Fencer said. "Those Endermen have everyone pretty spooked. What are we going to do?"

"Carver and I were just talking about that." Gameknight turned and found the NPC walking away from the well, toward a shadowy spot next to the wall. He waved at him to approach. "Carver, come over here."

Now it was Farmer's turn to scowl.

"I don't think we need Carver's input," Farmer said. "We need to decide what is best for the entire village. Carver's thoughts aren't needed."

Gameknight looked at Carver's face and could see anger and resignation. It was clear the big villager was used to being excluded, but that was not acceptable to the User-that-is-not-a-user.

"I think Carver's ideas will be useful to hear," Gameknight said.

Farmer frowned, but he didn't object further.

"Carver, based on what you heard from the Endermen, what do you think we should do?" Gameknight asked.

"Well—" he started, but Farmer interrupted.

"We need to finish these walls and towers, and then they won't be able to touch us," Farmer said. "We'll be safe behind our walls."

"The walls won't protect us from those Endermen," Carver pointed out.

"Gameknight said he can show us how to fight them," the aged leader replied.

"But we can't just sit here and wait for this Herobrine and his army of monsters to descend down upon us," Carver said, getting angry. "We need to go out and face him in a place where *we* have the advantage."

"Well said, Carver," Gameknight added. "I think he's right. I've learned one thing while fighting Herobrine and his monsters: If you stay stationary, then you'll be defeated. Mobility and the element of surprise are the keys to success."

"Then what is it you think we should do?" Farmer asked, casting an annoyed glance at Carver.

"We need information," Gameknight said. "That zombie we caught said Herobrine had a group of monsters collecting at Dragon's Teeth. I think we need to go there and see what the monsters are doing."

"You want to go looking for a monster army?" Farmer asked, astonished. "That sounds kinda crazy."

"A danger that is seen is a danger that can be avoided," the User-that-is-not-a-user said. "We must know what's going on, and the only way to do that is to go to Dragon's Teeth."

"I'll go with you, Smithy," Carver said.

"Thank you, Carver, but we'll need more than just a few of us," Gameknight said.

"SMITHY!" came a cry from the villagers who had been edging closer to the discussion and eavesdropping.

"Well, OK," Farmer said hesitantly.

"The wounded should stay here and the builders must continue on the wall. We want Herobrine to think we're *all* still here, and not spying on him," Gameknight explained. "I can take a group of maybe fifty warriors. Carver, do you know how to get to this Dragon's Teeth?"

The big NPC nodded his head.

"Farmer, you stay here and keep everyone working. We want to make sure Herobrine thinks we're all here, and the only way to do that is to have a lot of people on the walls, keeping busy and building." Gameknight turned to Carver. "Pick the warriors you want. We'll need villagers good with the bow and the sword. Who knows what we'll run into out there?"

Carver cast Gameknight a wry grin, then moved about the village, identifying those that would accompany them.

The User-that-is-not-a-user turned and faced Weaver.

"I want you and the other kids to stay here," Gameknight said in a stern voice. "Do you understand?"

"But we could help . . ." the young villager complained.

Gameknight moved closer to the boy and spoke in a low voice.

"I don't like the way their butcher has been looking at Wilbur," the User-that-is-not-a-user said. "I need you to watch out for my friend and make sure no one is gonna eat him. Can I rely on you to do this?"

"Oink," the little animal said when he heard his name.

Weaver sighed, then nodded his head.

"This is important to me," Gameknight added. "I'm putting Wilbur's life in your hands. Will you make sure no one in the village does anything to him?"

"I guarantee it," Weaver said with a smile.

He didn't like that smile.

"You and all the other kids are responsible for this," Gameknight said.

"I got it, you can trust me," Weaver said.

"OK," he replied.

Turning, he saw Carver walking toward the village gates with fifty heavily-armed warriors following behind him. Every one wore leather armor and had a bow in their hands. Carver cast Gameknight a smile, glared at Farmer as he passed, and led the warriors out of the village.

"Fencer, I'll be back as quickly as possible," the User-that-is-not-a-user said. "Make sure the village is ready for any attack from Herobrine."

"We'll be ready, Smithy," he replied with a grin.

Gameknight glanced at Weaver. The young NPC gave him a suspicious smile and waved, then knelt and patted Wilbur on the back. Turning, the User-that-is-not-a-user had an uneasy feeling about this expedition. He knew they had to find out what Herobrine was doing, but he still felt like they were walking into trouble, and there was nothing he could do about it.

## CHAPTER 11

# CREEPERS

**H**erobrine smiled an evil smile as he surveyed his territory. He stood atop the rocky spire spewing a wonderful flow of lava. The thick, molten stone oozed its way down the side of the mountain, filling the air with ash and acrid smoke; it smelled wonderful. Across from him, another mountaintop wept a stream of water that cascaded down its side, splitting into two separate waterfalls that crashed to the ground. The remaining two Teeth were bare, except for the snow that covered all the exposed flat surfaces near their peaks.

Below him, monsters approached the landmark from all directions. Zombies and skeletons shuffled in from the east, though not very many of them were coming now. Their eyes nervously shifted up to the sun overhead. The decaying zombies and rattling skeletons hated being out in the sunlight. Before Herobrine's arrival to Minecraft, they would have burst into flames with exposure to sunlight, but the evil virus had modified the monsters's code, making them impervious to the light of day; it was how he'd bonded them to him.

The monsters dragged their feet across the rough stone ground, their bodies clearly fatigued. They'd drained this biome of its monsters for the first battle with the blacksmith; few still remained out there in the wild. Those that were not part of that fateful conflict were now coming to Dragon's Teeth from far away, answering Herobrine's call. Giving off sorrowful moans, the zombies walked slowly across the rocky landscape, their arms extended out in front of them. Herobrine didn't really understand why they had to put their arms out, as they looked silly doing it; it must have been something in their programming, for they all did it.

The skeletons were another matter. These pale, white creatures could control their arms while they walked, but they were unable to quiet the constant clattering of their bones as they rattled together. They all held a bow in their hands but were inherently poor shots. Herobrine hoped that Skeletonbrine, the shadow-crafter responsible for improving the skeletons, could help with that. He had made this a priority for Skeletonbrine, making sure the shadow-crafter understood his very existence depended upon his success.

Just then, a large group of creepers emerged from the birch forest to the south, as well as from the desert to the north. Oxus, the creeper king, had put out a call to his creepers, and the mottled green monsters were arriving in waves. The idiotic monsters had been nearly worthless in the first battle of the Great Zombie Invasion, failing to detonate on command. Now, Creeperbrine had guaranteed Herobrine that this problem could be solved. He hoped that his shadow-crafter was correct; he didn't want to have to destroy him and make another if he failed, but he made it clear to the creature that he was willing to do so.

Mixed in with the creepers were the spiders that Shaikulud was gathering for her Maker. The fuzzy black arachnids had been difficult to see in the darkness of the night, their multiple bright red eyes the only thing visible as they moved. But now, in the full light of day, the shadowy monsters were easy to spot against the gray stone that made up the extreme hills biome.

Below, Herobrine could see the monster kings and queen gathering near the entrance to their underground hideaway. At the speed of thought, the shadowy Maker disappeared, then reappeared near his commanders.

"Oxus, you have done well bringing me these creepers, but there is still more to do," Herobrine said.

"What is it that the Maker commands?" the creeper king asked.

"I have a plan for the creepers that may end this war quicker and save many monster lives."

Oxus's eyes grew bright at the sound of saving monster lives. "What are your orders?" he hissed, his body glowing bright as he spoke.

"You have served me well by bringing all of these creepers here to me," Herobrine said. "But we still need more, and I fear you have exhausted the supply of creepers in this area."

Oxus nodded his green head in agreement.

"Therefore, you are commanded to go far from here and bring even more of your creepers," Herobrine continued. "I need hundreds of your brothers and sisters if we are to end this war and protect the lives of monsters, and no time can be spared. The monsters you have brought me will be put to use as necessary, but we cannot launch our final assault on the blacksmith without more. Is this understood?"

Oxus nodded again as blue and red sparks danced across his body, remnants from when Herobrine had created him.

"Go now, and do not return until you have collected your creeper army," the evil virus commanded.

Oxus turned and scurried across the stone ground, his tiny pig-like green feet a blur as he headed off to the southeast in search of his kind.

Next, Herobrine turned to Shaikulud.

"What issss your command?" the spider queen said.

"I want a company of your spiders to patrol the birch forest to the south," Herobrine said. "The surviving zombie said he encountered a group of villagers in that biome. I need your spiders to watch our southern border. We cannot let the blacksmith see what we are doing here. When we fall upon him and his pathetic villagers, the size of our army will be such a surprise that many of his NPCs will likely just die of fright."

Erebus laughed, his red eyes glowing bright.

"Shaikulud, you will stay here while your sisters go forth," Herobrine ordered. "I want *you* to collect more spiders for me. We need our numbers to be overwhelming, and your spiders are an important part of my army. With your new strength and power, compliments of Spiderbrine, your sisters will be more vicious than ever, but still we need greater numbers. You *must* bring me more monsters. Do you understand?"

"Yessss, Maker," she hissed.

"Bring me the monsters that I need, and we will be victorious," Herobrine added.

"The cave underground issss becoming crowded," the spider queen pointed out. "We will need more room ssssoon."

"Don't worry about that," her Maker said. "For now, all I need you to do is watch for the villagers and continue to command your spiders to come here, to Dragon's Teeth."

"I undersssstand, Maker," Shaikulud said.

"Very good, now go!"

The spider closed her purple eyes for just an instant. Herobrine knew she was sending out psychic commands to her spiders. A group of the fuzzy monsters crawled out of the dark hole that sat between the Teeth of the Dragon, and moved to her, their wicked, curved claws clicking on the hard stone. When they drew near, the spider queen opened her angry purple eyes and nodded to Herobrine. Clicking their mandibles together excitedly, the tiny army of arachnids headed to the south, toward the birch forest that bordered the extreme hills biome, their multiple red eyes glowing with evil excitement.

# CHAPTER 12

# CARVER

According to Farmer, Dragon's Teeth was on the other side of the Great Chasm, and few NPCs ever visited the place. Monsters were rumored to gather there, meaning it was not safe for villagers, but Farmer could remember going to it before the . . . Awakening. He knew it could only be reached by either heading north and going around the end of the Chasm, or heading southeast to go across the bridge and then approaching the Teeth from the south. Knowing that the birch forest sat at the end of the bridge, Gameknight chose the latter so they could stay under cover and hopefully remain unseen.

Carver, again, led the party through the desert toward the Midnight Bridge. The group moved across the sandy terrain in complete silence, except for the slap of their leather armor and the thud of heavy boots on the dry ground. The perpetual east-to-west breeze made the occasional dried shrub rustle and shake, but little else moved in the desert. It was deathly quiet, and that made the NPCs nervous. As a precaution, Gameknight sent scouts out ahead to make sure there were no surprises waiting for them; he also sent a few to the rear, just to be sure nothing was following. Some of the NPCs rolled their eyes, thinking it was unnecessary, but Gameknight had learned many times over never to underestimate Herobrine and his thirst for violence.

Soon, the Great Chasm came into view. In the full light of the afternoon sun, it looked like an angry black slash in the pale landscape, but as they neared, Gameknight could see light at the bottom of the steep ravine. Lava poured out of numerous holes, lighting the floor with a bright orange glow. A few monsters moved about, which was strange; he'd expected to see more. They only spotted a couple of spiders and one lone zombie.

"That doesn't make sense," Gameknight said, his voice breaking the silence and easing the tension.

"What?" Fencer asked.

"There are almost no monsters down there," Gameknight said. "They must be somewhere, and I'd feel a lot better knowing where they were."

"You want *more* monsters?" Fencer said. "Smithy be crazy."

The other villagers chuckled softly. Gameknight shrugged, then gave them a smile.

"Carver, how long have you lived in that desert village?" the User-that-is-not-a-user asked.

"Why do you assume I wasn't born there?" the stocky NPC asked.

"I see a lot of sand around, but not very much wood to carve. It's likely that the village doesn't have a huge need for a carver. You see, I've learned that the environment seems to drive the kind of villagers that are born in a community. A desert village would need a lot of farmers for crops and builders for homes, but everything is made of sandstone, and there's no wood in sight."

Carver sighed and became very quiet. An uneasy silence spread through the other NPCs. They became very tense and cast cautious glances toward Carver, as if expecting him to explode in a rage.

"I've heard this a million times through my life. Why are you here, what do you do for the village, what good are you?" Carver growled, trying to keep his voice down, but anger and frustration were bubbling to the surface. "I have an axe for carving; it's my prized possession, yet I have nothing to carve. All I ever wanted to do was carve with this axe. It is my purpose in life . . . I know it. But in the eyes of the village elders, I'm worthless and insignificant. All of the men in my family, my uncles, my dad, my brother . . . they are all bakers, except for me. I'm the misfit, the reject . . . the carver."

"I'm sorry, I didn't know," Gameknight said.

"It doesn't matter. I've heard it all before," Carver continued. "Instead of carving wood, which is the only thing I've ever wanted to do, I work in the village mines, smashing rocks with a pickaxe."

"Being a miner is an honorable profession," Gameknight said.

"I know," Carver snapped, then cast his green eyes to the ground. "There is something out there that I must carve with my axe, but I cannot ever seem to find it, and because of that, I feel empty inside. I always keep my axe razor-sharp, just in case I find what I need, but I've never found the right piece of wood to use it on. In fact, I've never used the axe on *any* wood. Because of that, I can't even chop down a tree. So not only am I not needed in the village, but I can't even use my axe for something useful to help my fellow NPCs." His head drooped as he shuffled his feet across the sand. "I'm nothing but an empty shell."

"Carver, I know what you are feeling," Gameknight said.

"How can you know how I am feeling? You're the great Smithy, now Smithy of the Two-Swords. You have purpose coming out of your ears."

"Yes, but it hasn't always been like that," Gameknight said as he moved next to the big NPC and lowered his voice. "There was a time when I struggled for acceptance and doubted my self-worth. I was depressed and questioned my value, and I believed everyone would be better off without me."

"That's a really inspiring pep-talk," Carver said.

Gameknight smiled. "That would be something an old friend, Hunter, might say to me. You'd like her."

Carver said nothing.

"What I learned from Hunter, and some of my other friends, is that as you go through life, you'll always be looking for that thing that completes you, that resonates with your soul so profoundly that it makes you finally feel alive. And when you find that thing, you can't even imagine how you ever lived without it."

"Again, not a big help."

Gameknight ignored him and continued.

"I found that for me, it was my friends. They completed me, and made me feel like I was part of a family," Gameknight explained. "And I would do anything to help them, even fight in this crazy war against Herobrine. I'd do anything to make sure they were OK, and I wouldn't quit until I was successful. I feel content that I finally found that thing that fills my soul, and I'm grateful every day for finding it.

"Everyone has that thing, that missing piece to your soul. You just have to be willing to keep looking for it, for if you give up, then you will always feel incomplete."

Gameknight placed a hand on the big villager's shoulder.

"Have faith, Carver. There are those around here that care about you and want to see you find that thing as much as you want to find it. Just don't give up."

Carver turned and looked at Gameknight, his deep, green eyes filled with a faint spark of hope. He nodded his head, then reached into his inventory and pulled out his axe, his hand sliding along its stout handle. Just then, one of the scouts returned.

"The Bridge . . . it's just ahead," he said. "We didn't see any monsters about. Come on."

The villagers started to run, following the scout. They curved their way around the tall, prickly green cactuses and jumped over the dried shrubs as the desert grew dark. The sun was just beginning to kiss the horizon, throwing splashes of color across the pale landscape. The last time they'd been here, it had been night. But this time, there was enough light to see the bridge ahead. It was awe-inspiring. Whoever had built this structure had put incredible detail into it, detail that had not been visible in the middle of the night. Tiny features, like Nether brick fencing along the edges of the tall columns and dark oak steps beneath the supports, added a meticulous touch that made it obviously the work of a building master.

They reached the near end of the bridge and moved across, just as the shadow of night touched the far side. The fifty warriors squeezed into the three-block wide pathway, moving across the long bridge as quickly as possible. But just as they reached the midpoint, a clicking sound, like that of a thousand crickets, filled the air ahead.

Gameknight came to a stop, drawing his sword.

"Spiders," he whispered as Fencer drew his own blade as well and moved to his friend's side.

Gameknight glanced behind at the other villagers. They had nervous expressions on their square faces, but they continued across the bridge, following closely as their leader moved forward cautiously across the second half of the structure.

The clicking sounds grew louder. Gameknight glanced around, looking for the source, but saw nothing. Suddenly, the sounds came from behind and were increasing in volume. Jolts of fear electrified his nerves as the User-that-is-not-a-user glanced back to the other side of the bridge. A group of spiders scurried over a sand dune like a deadly wave, congregating over the end, destroying any thought of retreat.

"Look, they're up ahead as well," Fencer said, pointing.

Gameknight turned back to the front, only to find another group of monsters clogging the other end of the bridge. Their red eyes glowed bright in the dimming light of dusk, but one of the creatures stood apart from the rest, one with an icy purple gaze.

"Shaikulud," Gameknight hissed.

"What?" Carver asked.

"The spider queen," he said, pointing with his sword. "She has us trapped."

Carver said nothing, but gripped the handle of his sword as tightly as he could, a look of fear in his eyes. Gameknight glanced at the other soldiers around them and saw the same look: panic.

*I've led them into a trap*, Gameknight thought. *What a stupid thing to do! The real Smithy would have never been so foolish. These villagers need a real leader.*

Cold fingers of dread wrapped around his soul and squeezed, making him shudder as the reality of their impending defeat dawned on him.

The spiders began to move across the bridge, clicking their mandibles as they carefully approached. Fencer moved to the back of the army to face the monsters closing in from the rear, a grim look of determination etched into his square face.

Somehow, Gameknight needed to figure a way out of this trap or they would all be destroyed. The problem was, he was just as scared as the rest of them, and had no ideas. They couldn't run, and they likely they wouldn't be able to fight very well trapped in the middle of the bridge. All the User-that-is-not-a-user could think to do was stand there and wait for the inevitable.

# CHAPTER 13

# THE GREAT CHASM

The spiders charged forward, their multiple red eyes glowing bright in the darkness. Their bodies seemed to melt into the bridge as the setting sun drew the blanket of night across the heavens and their fuzzy abdomens blended in against the obsidian.

"Some of you, hold your position here and watch the spiders up ahead," Gameknight said, gritting his teeth. "The rest, come with me and watch the monsters at the rear."

He pushed his way through the warriors until he was standing at the back of the formation. With his two swords out, Gameknight was about to take a step forward when he noticed Carver at his side. The big NPC had an iron sword out and was waiting patiently, a grim look of determination on his square face. But as the monsters moved forward, some of them climbed up onto the sweeping curves of dark stone extending high into the air, the simulated cables of the bridge now giving the monsters access overhead.

"This is not good," Carver said. "Now they can drop right down on top of us."

Gameknight quickly counted. He estimated at least thirty of the creatures approaching from the rear, and at least that many coming at them from the front as well.

"We're surrounded and outnumbered," someone said.

"What do we do?" another cried.

"We should run . . ."

Everyone was yelling out what to do, but no one knew for sure. They needed a plan.

*Can I get them out of this?* Gameknight thought. *They need a real leader, like Smithy, not me . . . what* should *we do?*

"We're too close to fight, we need to spread out . . ."

"We can't, the bridge is too narrow!" someone shouted.

*Too narrow . . . of course!* Quickly, Gameknight put away his swords and pulled out blocks of stone. "Carver, with me!" the User-that-is-a-user shouted.

Ignoring the curious looks from the other villagers, he moved to the edge of the bridge and began placing down blocks of stone. Inching to the precipice, he placed more blocks, creating a platform on one side.

"What are you doing?" Carver asked.

Gameknight didn't even bother to look up.

"Place blocks on the edge and create a platform so we can fight."

The NPC didn't reply, immediately leaping into action. Gathering more villagers, Carver gave direction as Gameknight continued to place blocks. The villagers at the edges of the formation pulled out their bows and tried to keep the spiders back, but there were so many of them; there were too few villagers to slow the monsters significantly.

In under a minute, the platforms were built. NPCs now spread out across the new structures and waited, the extra room giving them more space to fight. The first wave of spiders reached them. Some of the fuzzy creatures lowered down on strands of silk, while others charged directly at them.

"Protect each other," Gameknight called out. "Watch each other's backs."

Spider claws slashed through the darkness, tearing into leather armor as if it was paper.

"These spiders seem stronger, somehow," Carver said at Gameknight's side. "They usually aren't this tough to beat."

"I know," the User-that-is-not-a-user replied.

It was true; the monsters were undeniably faster and more lethal. Herobrine must have done something to them . . . but what?

"There's too many of them," someone shouted. "We can't fight them from the front and rear at the same time!"

"What do we do, Smithy? What do we do?"

Suddenly, arrows began flying through the air from the end of the bridge. At the same time, an *Oink!* echoed across the Chasm.

"What was that?" Carver asked.

Gameknight turned and saw a group of villagers at the far end of the bridge, with a lone pig standing defiantly in the front. Another wave of arrows flew through the air from the new army of NPCs, then they charged forward.

"FOR MINECRAFT!" they yelled.

"It's Weaver and the other kids from the village!" Carver said.

"Weaver?!" Gameknight growled.

The kids ran toward the spiders, some with their swords held out so they could bang them against the bridge supports, causing an earth-shattering ruckus as they charged. There were maybe thirty of them, many still firing their bows as fast as they could. The spiders to the rear felt the sting of their shafts and turned to face the new threat.

"Some of you, reinforce those facing the spiders at the front. The rest, with me . . . ATTACK!" Gameknight yelled.

With the spiders facing away, the NPCs fell upon them. With his two swords shining in the moonlight, the User-that-is-not-a-user dove into the formation, slashing at spiders to the left and right. His blades were a blur as he moved from one target to the next.

Behind him, Gameknight could hear the warriors at the front of the bridge in a pitched battle with the monsters. Cries of pain and fright came from both villagers and spiders as the battle raged. The fuzzy monsters before him tried to step back to regain their position, but there was no place for them to go. Now the spiders were trapped between two forces.

Quickly, the monsters' numbers diminished. Gameknight carved away at their HP while the group led by Weaver smashed into piles of arachnids. Glancing over his shoulder, the User-that-is-not-a-user saw Carver at the edge of the spider formation. He was slashing at the spiders frantically, with Builder and Planter at his side. Gameknight thought the stocky NPC looked clumsy with the sword, as if the weapon didn't belong in his hand for some reason.

A spider claw suddenly scraped across his leggings, tearing a deep gash into the leather and narrowly missing the flesh protected underneath. Gameknight spun and drove his swords into the creature, scoring a quick succession of critical hits that made the monster flash red as it took damage. With Carver and his warriors at one side, and Weaver's group at the other, the spiders quickly fell until they were all gone.

Without pause, Gameknight turned and charged toward the other end of the bridge. The villagers that stayed on the platform were battling for their lives, outnumbered and facing a dangerous foe. But as the warriors closed in on the monsters, the spiders fought harder. It was clear they were not going to retreat.

"Weaver, quickly build some towers. Use the overhead supports."

The young boy glanced upward, then nodded. He pulled out blocks of stone and constructed a small tower that would allow him to get above the warriors. With the help of the other kids, they made a wide cobblestone tower from which they could shoot down at the fighting creatures.

Their bows began to hum as arrows rained down upon the spiders, causing the black, fuzzy bodies to flash red with damage. Between the swords and the arrows, the spiders quickly fell.

"Don't let any escape," Gameknight said. "Charge!"

The warriors pushed forward, shoving spiders off the bridge to plummet to their doom. Finally, the last of the fuzzy monsters perished with a *pop*.

Glancing around him, Gameknight could see the piles of items left behind, marking where villagers had perished. Many had not survived because of his leadership. A heaviness settled in his heart as he thought about those poor souls, sadness and guilt filling his inner being. Slowly, he raised his hand into the air, fingers spread. The other NPCs saw this and followed his example, offering a salute for the dead. Gameknight spread his fingers wide, then clenched them into a fist and squeezed tight.

"We will not let our friends' deaths be in vain," Gameknight said as he lowered his hand.

He growled at Weaver and gave him an angry scowl. But then Wilbur came running across the bridge, oinking as he approached.

"I told you I'd keep my eye on him," Weaver said.

"Bringing everyone here was dangerous!" Gameknight snapped. "You should have listened to me. Some of these kids could have been hurt. *You* could have been hurt."

"We knew we could handle it. And besides, if we hadn't come along, all of you would have been in trouble. So I guess we saved the day, huh? It all turned out OK."

"The ends do not justify the means," Gameknight growled. "I told you to stay at the village for your safety and you ignored me!"

He turned away from the boy and stared down into the Chasm, furious at Weaver.

"I'm sorry, Smithy," Weaver said. "It's just that all the villagers say we can't do anything, that we're too small and too young. But they're wrong. We can do a lot of things to help and we're tired of just being ignored and treated like we're worthless."

"I get it, kid," Carver said. *"I'm* glad you came along."

"Carver, you're not helping," Gameknight said.

The stocky NPC just shrugged.

Gameknight knelt before Weaver and spoke quietly. "I need you to listen to me so that I can keep you safe. Do you understand that?"

"Yeah, I guess," Weaver replied.

He reached out and tussled his hair, then patted Wilbur on the head. Whatever the circumstances, seeing his friend and pig always lifted Gameknight's spirits.

"Alright then. Come on, let's see what Herobrine is up to."

Turning, he sprinted across Midnight Bridge and toward Dragon's Teeth.

## CHAPTER 14

# ZOMBIE-TOWNS

The large group of zombies shuffled forward through the forest, nervously glancing over their shoulders. Their sorrowful moans were filled with an extra dose of fear as they strained to move fast enough to avoid punishment.

"You zombies are under my command whether you like it or not," Herobrine growled. "Hiding in dark caves and tunnels will not allow you to escape my sight. I can see and feel everything in Minecraft."

He had sensed these zombies cowering underground, unwilling to answer his call and come to Dragon's Teeth to join his army. As an example to the rest of his army, Herobrine had destroyed a dozen of the decaying monsters, just so that the others knew that the consequences of disobeying his commands would be severe. It worked; after the executions, the remaining zombies had been happy to lend their claws to his war. But just to be certain, Herobrine had escorted them all to the surface, ushering them toward the Teeth as if they were a herd of cattle. Any monsters that strayed too far from the rest were greeted by the sharp point of his sword, encouraging all of the zombies to stay together and move quickly.

Soon, Herobrine could smell the smoke and ash from the lava that flowed down the side of one of the Teeth. It smelled wonderful and brought a devious smile to his square face.

"Hurry up!" the Maker snapped. "The last one to make it to Dragon's Teeth will be thrown in the lava."

The zombies shuffled faster; it made Herobrine laugh.

Suddenly, a purple cloud of mist formed next to him. Instantly, Erebus materialized by Herobrine's side.

"Maker, welcome back," the king of the Endermen said. "I see there are more zombies . . . excellent. But there is little room for them all in the caves."

"I felt a large group of creepers arrive recently," Herobrine said.

"Yes, they are here."

"We will put them to work, then, to help with our space problem," Herobrine ordered. "Now, have one of your Endermen escort these zombies to Dragon's Teeth. Whichever one arrives last is to be punished . . . by death!"

"Understood," Erebus said.

The Endermen king disappeared, then reappeared seconds later with another shadowy monster at his side.

"This Enderman will make sure the zombies make it to our base," Erebus said.

"Excellent. Now, meet me at the cave opening," Herobrine said.

At the speed of thought, the evil maker appeared next to the hole that sat between the four Dragon's

Teeth. An instant later, the dark red Erebus materialized at his side.

Herobrine stepped to the edge of the gaping hole that plunged downward into the ground. The four spires that made up Dragon's Teeth climbed high into the night sky close around the entrance to the hole, as if guarding it with their rocky fangs. The landscape, lit from the orange glow of the molten stone that bled down the side of one of the spires, had an eerie look to it, like the scene from some kind of terrible nightmare . . . it was wonderful.

Peering into the shadowy passage, Herobrine could see that it went down a dozen blocks or so, then turned and extended horizontally. Steps had been carefully carved into the tunnel walls, making it easy for monsters to enter and leave, but at the moment many of the monsters were milling about outside the chamber; there was clearly not enough room for all of them underground.

Moving closer to the edge of the tunnel, Herobrine peered down into the darkness, then turned and glared at the creepers standing around.

"Get down there, you idiotic creepers!" Herobrine growled, even though he knew they couldn't. There was nothing the evil virus liked more than making unreasonable demands.

He glanced at a group of Endermen and some newly arrived blazes.

"Endermen, help them, now! Blazes, you get down there as well. Don't make me wait."

He glared at them, his eyes glowing bright. With an angry scowl painted on his face, Herobrine waited as a group of blazes floated past, followed by a stream of creepers jumping from step to step as they descended down underground. He materialized at the bottom of the vertical section, where the tunnel bent and extended horizontally. He could see that it stretched forward, probably another twenty blocks or so, before it ended at a blank, rocky wall. Slowly, the smell of ash and smoke filled the air. Glancing over his shoulder, Herobrine saw the blazes approaching from behind.

"Wait next to me," Herobrine commanded. The flaming creatures complied, the spinning blaze rods that made up their bodies glowing in the darkness.

Suddenly, a mist of purple teleportation particles formed near one wall, and then an Enderman appeared, holding a creeper with each arm. The mottled green creatures looked terrified for a moment, but when they felt something solid under their piglike feet, the explosive monsters relaxed and began to scurry about. The Enderman disappeared, then returned with more of the green monsters. Finally, Erebus appeared with two more creepers in tow. He moved next to his Maker.

"Creepers, go to that wall and stand there," Herobrine commanded. The monsters moved to the wall, not giving the order any thought.

"All the way against the wall," he added. The monsters moved up against the stone edge of the tunnel.

The evil shadow-crafter gestured to the blaze and nodded his head. Instantly, balls of flame streaked out from the fiery monster and struck the creeper. The green monster began to hiss and glow brightly, swelling a bit, then detonated, tearing into the wall and carving more space into the cavern.

"Perfect," Herobrine said, chuckling. He glanced up at the Erebus. "The creepers will obey you and all your Endermen. I want a massive cavern carved into the flesh of Minecraft, right here. It must be bigger than any cave you can imagine. Do you understand?"

Erebus nodded his dark crimson head.

"Use as many of the creepers as necessary," Herobrine said. "We must make room for *real* monsters. Put one of your trusted Endermen in charge and make sure they do this right, then meet me above."

Without waiting for a response, the evil Herobrine teleported from the cavern and back to the surface. In moments, Erebus was again at his side.

"Endermen, gather," the Maker commanded.

The dark creatures instantly disappeared, then materialized before him in a cloud of purple mist. Herobrine addressed the congregation of shadowy monsters.

"I have created HP fountains all across the Overworld. They are hidden in caves deep within the extreme hills biomes. If you listen carefully to Minecraft, you can hear them." He paused as the Endermen all tilted their heads slightly, listening; many began to nod. "Teleport to those locations. Take many creepers with you, as well as a handful of blazes. The creepers will be used to carve out massive caverns for the zombies that will soon arrive. The decaying monsters can feel the pull of the HP fountains. You must make the cavern large enough to accommodate *a lot* of monsters. Understood?"

"What do you require from me?" Erebus asked.

"You will stay here and supervise the zombie-town below us, then set up defenses in case the villagers are foolish enough to attack."

"Where are you going, Maker?" the king of the Endermen asked.

"I am going forth to collect more monsters. Every zombie, skeleton, spider, and creeper will be forced to join our cause, or be destroyed."

He drew his sword in a quick, fluid motion. The iron blade gleamed with a bright orange glow, the light from the lava flow glistening off the weapon.

"Soon, we will have a massive army that will strike fear into every villager in the Overworld." He closed his eyes and reached out into Minecraft with his viral senses. "I can feel a huge contingent of creepers coming this way. They are easy to sense when they are on the surface." He closed his eyes and reached out into the fabric of Minecraft. "You will be surprised by how many creepers are coming to us. There are hundreds; Oxus did well."

Herobrine opened his eyes again.

"Shaikulud is doing the same. Soon, we will have an unstoppable force that will cover the surface of Minecraft with destruction."

Erebus began to cackle a high-pitched, screechy laugh, his eyes glowing a bright red.

"The infestation of villagers that has taken root all throughout the Overworld will be eradicated," Herobrine said. "When we are done, the world will belong to the monsters."

The Endermen nearby began to cackle like Erebus, all of their eyes glowing bright.

"Endermen, go and carry out my orders," Herobrine commanded. "Build me my zombie-towns and prepare for the multitudes arriving soon."

The dark monsters disappeared in puffs of purple mist, reappearing next to the large group of creepers. Each grabbed two of the mottled green creatures with their long, dark arms and teleported away with them. In minutes, nearly all of the creepers were gone. Herobrine watched the creatures disappear. An evil smile crept across his boxy face.

"Soon, blacksmith, I will have a surprise for you and all your pathetic villagers!"

And then Herobrine, too, disappeared from sight, leaving Dragon's Teeth filled with the awful cacophony of subterranean explosions.

# CHAPTER 15

# DRAGON'S TEETH

**C**arver led the way through the birch forest, keeping the Great Chasm just on their left and moving parallel to its crooked path. With the dim light from the half moon and the thick forest canopy overhead, it was as dark as a roofed forest. Which meant that a group of spiders could easily merge with the darkness and be impossible to see before it was too late . . .

However, Gameknight knew the spiders couldn't resist snapping their sharp mandibles together, making that telltale clicking sound that always announced the monsters before they arrived. So, moving in complete silence, the army kept an open ear out for the clicking beasts. Fortunately, either they avoided the terrible creatures, or the monsters weren't out looking for them.

Soon, they came upon the torches that Gameknight had placed in the ground on their previous trip, when the four of them were surrounded by zombies.

"Smithy, how do you think Herobrine made the spiders back there at the bridge so much stronger?" Fencer asked.

"I don't know," the User-that-is-not-a-user whispered. "Herobrine has special powers that his artificially intelligent viral computer code gives him. He is continually unpredictable."

"Whatever he did, I wish there was some way to even things up a bit and level the playing field," Fencer said.

"Me, too," Gameknight replied. "If *all* the monsters are that much stronger, then we're in trouble."

He thought he heard a sound at the back of the army.

"Fencer, come with me," Gameknight said.

The two of them stepped out of the formation and moved to the back of the army. Many of the warriors gave them confused looks, but Fencer just waved them forward. When they reached the rear, Gameknight stood still and listened intently. The sound of rustling leather armor and boots swishing through the long grass filled his ears, but nothing else.

"I thought I heard something back here," Gameknight said. "Guess not."

"Just your imagination again," Fencer replied. "Come on, let's catch up."

They turned and walked forward, following the crushed grass the group of NPCs left in their wake. While they walked, Gameknight turned to Fencer.

"Fencer, I think this thing with Herobrine is escalating," Gameknight said.

"What do you mean?"

"You know, the spiders getting deadlier," the User-that-is-not-a-user said. "Who knows what we'll face next. We'll have to get better weapons and armor, because I think the monsters will be getting meaner and more violent. It's an arms race, and I'm not sure if I'm the best person to be leading the villagers. I think I should come forward and reveal my true identity."

"The only thing keeping all the NPCs together is Smithy," Fencer said quietly. "If you tell the truth now, it will destroy everyone's faith and courage."

"But we'll have to eventually, right?" Gameknight asked. "I don't feel good about lying to everyone. It will just make coming clean that much more difficult."

"Trust me," Fencer said. "I was with Smithy a long time, even before the Awakening. All he ever did was care for others and make sure everyone was safe. You are doing the same thing, just in a different way. This is a good thing you're doing."

"How can telling a lie be a good thing?"

"Because you're saving the lives of countless NPCs," Fencer said, his voice growing in volume.

"Shhh," one of the warriors said at the back of the formation.

"Sorry," Fencer whispered. They slowed and moved a little farther from the others.

"I just think we need a plan," Gameknight said. "I don't feel good about lying to these villagers. They're good people, and deserve respect and truth."

"Fine, but not yet," Fencer whispered. "Just trust me. I'll tell you when it's a good time, and then you can blab it to the whole world."

"Well," Gameknight considered, and was about to object, when a voice came from the soldiers ahead of them.

"We're there," they said.

Gameknight and Fencer moved to the front of the group. Ahead, they could see four stone spires stretching up high into the sky. The orange glow of a massive lava flow lit the area as the thick molten stone slowly oozed down one spire, moving like thick, deadly honey. Another next to it was covered with two cascading waterfalls. Higher up on the steep mountains, the stone blocks were covered with a delicate frosting of snow, the actual peaks lost in a small group of clouds passing overhead.

Glancing up at the moon, the User-that-is-not-a-user estimated how long they had until sunrise.

"Here's what I want to do," he said. "We'll move through the forest under the cover of darkness, then approach Dragon's Teeth from the east."

"Why not just sneak up there now?" Fencer asked.

"If the light from that lava reflects off anything, we'll be spotted easily in the darkness," Gameknight explained. "If we approach from the east, at dawn, then we'll have the sun at our backs, and the monsters will have a harder time seeing us."

"I like that idea," Carver said. "The glare of the sun will blind any of the monsters that look in our direction, giving us the advantage."

The other NPCs nodded in agreement.

"But to do this, we need to move fast," Gameknight added. "If we get to the east side too late, then we're in big trouble, and the monsters will easily see us. It has to be timed just right."

"Leave it to Smithy to come up with a crazy plan like this," Weaver said. Gameknight glanced at him and grinned a devious grin. "Fencer said it earlier: 'Smithy be crazy!'"

The other NPCs chuckled, some of them slapping Gameknight on the back.

"Come on," the User-that-is-not-a-user said. "We need to be quick and quiet." He turned to Weaver. "Can you carry Wilbur?"

"No problem," the young NPC replied.

"OK . . . let's go."

They hustled quickly through the forest, weaving around trees and shrubs as they ran. Gameknight kept the glowing spires of Dragon's Teeth always in view as they moved beneath the leafy canopy. The army flowed through the forest like a silent, leathery tide. NPCs with the best eyesight were positioned on the periphery of the formation, keeping their eyes peeled for any movement from the rocky mountains. Fortunately, no monsters approached. By all indications, it seemed as if Herobrine did not know of their presence. Perfect.

Gameknight eyed the moon nervously during their sprint through the forest. By the time it was halfway to setting, the NPC army had made it through the forest and over a series of grass-covered hills, which ended in a narrow valley. Only the snowy tips of Dragon's Teeth were visible over the rise, their sharp, dagger-like peaks stabbing into the dark clouds drifting overhead. The group ran northward, racing the moon as they moved into position. With the rocky spires now directly to the west, the warriors slowly ascended the sloped side of the valley and peered up at the nearby mountains.

The sky behind them began to blush a deep crimson, a warning that the sun would be rising soon. It cast a warm glow upon the landscape, replacing the terror of the night with a feeling of serenity and hope. That was, until the moans of the zombies reached their ears.

Moving closer to Dragon's Teeth, Gameknight could see at least a hundred zombies shuffling about, large groups of spiders and skeletons mixed in with them. The assortment of monster bodies made for an awful kaleidoscope of color that blanketed the stone between the steep spires. It was at the same time beautiful and terrifying.

Beneath them, Gameknight could feel deep vibrations. The ground underfoot began to rumble with something that felt and sounded like subterranean explosions, the detonations muffled and barely audible. It felt as if the very fabric of Minecraft was shaking in fear.

"You see how many monsters they have out there?" Fencer said.

"More than I can count," Weaver replied.

"Maybe we should get out of here now," Fencer suggested nervously.

"Not yet. We need to get closer," Gameknight said. "All I can see are the monsters out there on the ground. We need to see if Herobrine has any defenses that will need to be dealt with."

*Closer?* Fencer mouthed to Weaver.

*Crazy,* the young NPC mouthed in return.

The small NPC army moved closer to Dragon's Teeth as the collection of monsters growled and moaned, filling the air with hatred.

# CHAPTER 16
# DISPOSABLE RESOURCES

**H**erobrine materialized at the top of one of the Dragon's Teeth and gazed down at his army. Below him, a massive group of monsters was arriving. Huge companies of zombies and skeletons shuffled toward the Teeth from the north, flowing around large hills and between the massive stone spires like a speckled green-and-white tide. Throughout the area could be heard the clattering bones of the skeletons and the sorrowful wails of the zombies.

To the west, a black wave of spiders was crawling out of the Great Chasm. They scuttled out of the deep ravine like a reverse flood, climbing the sheer walls with ease and spreading across the landscape like a dark blanket of angry red eyes and sharp claws. They moved straight into the hole in the ground that sat between the four mountains, hiding their numbers from any unwanted viewers.

Moving up from the south was a group of creepers. At the front of the emerald wave was a glowing green creature, waves of blue and red sparks dancing across the monster's body.

Teleporting to him, Herobrine materialized next to Oxus, the king of the creepers.

"You have brought many creepers with you," Herobrine said. "Excellent. They will be put to good use."

"There are more coming, many more," the creeper king said. "I think when you show all these creepers on the field of battle, it will cause the villagers to just surrender in fear."

Oxus waited for his glowing body to dim. Creepers spoke by starting their ignition process. The ordinary creeper needed to be careful; if they spoke too long, they could explode. This had the effect of making arguments either very short, or very explosively final. But for Oxus, he could speak without exploding—a gift from Herobrine during his making. This allowed the creeper king to use longer sentences.

"Having my creepers present will likely just stop all fighting and allow all of us to go back to our lives in peace," Oxus hissed in suggestion.

"Yes, of course," Herobrine said, the lie flowing easily past his lips. "That's what we all want, an end to violence so we can all go back to our lives. But for that to happen, I will need many more creepers. Once the creepers you have collected are safely tucked away in the zombie-town underground, then you are to go out and collect more of your brothers and sisters."

"Yes, Maker," the king of the creepers replied.

"Excellent," Herobrine replied.

Closing his eyes, he teleported at the speed of thought, materializing in the huge zombie-town beneath Dragon's Teeth. He could have just walked there, for a huge hole led underground to the secret cavern, but Herobrine refused to walk like these disposable monsters. He was far too important for something like that.

His army was growing larger and larger in the subterranean cavern. Soon, he would have sufficient numbers to attack that pathetic blacksmith and erase him from the face of Minecraft. But first, he wanted his army to be so vast that he could easily sacrifice many of the creatures, just to make the foolish blacksmith suffer.

Suddenly, a purple mist formed next to him. Erebus appeared within the cloud, his dark red skin making him stand out against the other Endermen in the cave.

"Maker, the progress on the zombie-towns is going well," the king of the Endermen said. "The blazes are using the creepers very efficiently, to get the most out of each monster's life when they explode."

"Excellent!" exclaimed Herobrine. "Now, I need you to supervise the shadow-crafters."

The Maker pointed to the far side of the cavern. There, surrounded by a ring of lava, sat the terrible shadow-crafters. Each had a monster of one type or another before them, their hands manipulating the creatures, making them stronger or faster or meaner.

"Be sure they understand: if they cannot improve my monsters, then they are of no use to me and can be disposed of."

"Yes, Maker," Erebus said, an excited look on his terrifying face.

"Harm none of them now," Herobrine ordered. "Wait for my command. So far, they have increased the strength of the zombies, made spiders run faster and fight harder, increased the accuracy of the skeletons, and made the creepers smarter. But I need more. They are to drive as much violent hatred into the monsters as possible.".

Herobrine's eyes began to glow white.

"When that puny blacksmith meets my monsters in battle again, he will be quite surprised. And with all the additional creepers that will arrive soon, victory is nearly guaranteed."

Erebus's eyes glowed a bright red as the thought of their impending victory filled his evil mind.

"Soon, my monsters will spread across the Overworld, destroying villages at will," Herobrine explained. "As soon as this pesky blacksmith is out of the way, then there will be no one to unify the NPCs. Nothing will be able to stand against us. And soon—"

Suddenly, an Enderman materialized right in front of Herobrine and Erebus.

"My King, Maker," the Enderman interrupted.

Herobrine's eyes glowed white with anger at being disturbed by this unimportant creature.

"You dare interrupt Herobrine!" the Maker exclaimed.

He reached for his sword and drew it slowly, the sharp edge scraping against its scabbard, creating a hissing noise that sounded like a massive viper.

"It's just that . . ." the Enderman took a step back. "Villagers . . . approaching . . . Dragon's Teeth," the dark monster stammered.

"What's this?" Herobrine asked.

"I posted Endermen around Dragon's Teeth as sentries," Erebus explained. "I didn't want any NPCs sneaking up on us."

"And this Enderman here spotted them?" Herobrine asked.

Erebus nodded.

"Excellent," Herobrine said, slapping the Enderman on the arm. It startled the dark creature so much that he disappeared, then materialized a dozen blocks away, shaking in fear.

"Erebus, it is time we tested our new monsters," the evil Maker said. "Let's see if these shadow-crafters are doing anything useful or not. It is time you commanded your army in battle."

"It would be my pleasure," Erebus said, then cackled a spine-tingling laugh that caused the monsters in zombie-town to shiver in fear.

## CHAPTER 17

# OLD FRIENDS REUNITED

Gameknight led the party of villagers closer to Dragon's Teeth as the bright light of the sun cast long shadows before each of them. The barren peaks stretched high up into the sky. Though the spires were only a few blocks wide at the summit, they were immense at the base.

Moving around the perimeter of one of the mountains, Gameknight could see huge groups of monsters walking to the center of the fang-like formation. They descended into a large hole that likely led to some kind of tunnel or cavern system. The number of monsters was frightening, but even worse: upon closer inspection, Gameknight could see that many of the monsters were creepers. That would be a big problem.

Deciding he'd seen enough, Gameknight slowly backed away, edging across a stone-covered clearing and toward the birch forest. But when they were almost to the edge of the woods, a growling sound filled the air.

"Zombie," Fencer whispered.

Gameknight quickly drew his swords and backed up slowly. The growling was getting louder, but now additional voices joined the first . . . there was more than one of them.

Suddenly, a group of decaying green monsters burst from the forest and charged across the clearing. Something about them was even more terrifying than usual. The zombies looked somehow meaner and stronger. They moved quickly towards the NPCS to attack. Charging straight toward him, the lead zombie lunged at Gameknight, its razor-sharp claws swiping across his chest, slicing easily through the leather tunic.

More villagers charged ahead, standing side-by-side as they stood their ground before the monsters.

"Move forward," Gameknight said. "Push them back."

The villagers attacked, the swordsmen slashing at the zombies, while archers fired their arrows from between NPC bodies. Many of the villagers yelled out in pain as zombie claws slashed through leather armor to the soft flesh beneath. Somehow, the monsters were stronger and more vicious than any of them could remember.

"Keep advancing," Gameknight said.

There were only a dozen of the monsters, and he had at least sixty warriors, counting the kids brought by Weaver; this battle should be easy. But the zombies continued to fight and gave little ground, their ferocity startling. The stinking creatures were wounding one villager after another. When one of the NPCs was hurt, they would step back and use their bow from afar as another took their place. But soon, all of the villagers were injured save for Gameknight999. And even though

the zombies were also wounded and losing the battle, they refused to retreat.

But slowly the decaying beasts fell. Finally,
they were all destroyed, and Gameknight glanced
around at his companions. He only saw a few piles
of items on the ground, thankfully, but the deaths
of the villagers hung heavy on his mind.

*Would the real Smithy have done any bet-
ter?* Gameknight thought. *Probably. Am I good
enough to lead these brave villagers? Or am I just
a fraud?*

Doubt circled through his mind as he stared
down at a leather tunic that hovered on the ground
near his feet. The brown armor was sliced to shreds,
and a discarded sword floating right nearby.

"We need to get out of here," Carver said, his
arm around a wounded villager.

"I agree," Fencer added.

"OK, let's go," Gameknight said.

He turned and peered back toward the mass
of monster bodies flowing into the dark hole that
sat between the rocky spires. Suddenly, the monsters stopped their descent and all turned their evil
heads directly toward the villagers.

"Oh, no," Gameknight moaned.

"They know we're here," Carver whispered. "We
need to get out of here, now."

The NPCs slowly retreated, trying to make as
little noise as possible.

"So, blacksmith, you've come to spy on me, have
you?" a voice cackled from behind.

Gameknight spun around and found Herobrine
standing at the edge of the birch forest. Around
him were fifty Endermen, as well as dozens of spiders and zombies and skeletons.

"I've been looking forward to meeting up with you again."

"I'm not afraid of you, Herobrine," Gameknight tried to snarl, but his voice cracked, exposing the fear that filled his whole being.

Herobrine laughed.

"Yes, I'm sure you're not afraid one bit."

He laughed again, causing the Endermen to chuckle. A screechy laugh cut through the rest. Gameknight would have recognized that evil voice anywhere, but still he prayed that he was wrong. Color drained from his face as he slowly turned his head toward the sound.

"Ahh, I see you've found my newest servant," Herobrine said with an evil grin. "Allow me to introduce to you the king of the Ender . . ."

"Erebus," Gameknight hissed. He was now shaking.

*It can't be . . . my nightmare has returned.* Gameknight thought. *How can I lead these villagers when I'm terrified of this one creature?*

He thought back to their last meeting, on the steps to the Source. He'd battled the dark monster in the land of dreams, but he'd had the help of both Hunter and Stitcher. Here, he felt utterly alone.

"I've been looking forward to meeting you, blacksmith," Erebus screeched. "Come, let us embrace."

The king of the Endermen laughed again.

More Endermen appeared around the villagers, each one with a zombie or a skeleton in its long, clammy arms. A massive group of spiders clicked anxiously, adding to the excited moans of the zombies and the clattering skeletons. Slowly, monsters moved around the base of one of the mountains, their cold, dead eyes all trained on the villagers with venomous hatred.

"Smithy, what do we do?" Carver asked. "We're outnumbered and surrounded . . . quick, tell us what to do."

Fencer moved to Gameknight's side and spoke in his ear.

"We need to do something, fast, or we're all lost. Quick, think of something. We need one of your unexpected tricks to get us out of this."

But Gameknight could not answer. He was terrified beyond all rational thought. Before him was his own personal nightmare, Erebus, the king of the Endermen. And now they were surrounded and outnumbered by at least three to one. They were lost and had no chance for success. Gameknight could think of only one thing to do. He reached into his inventory and drew his iron swords, and waited for the end to come crashing down upon them in a wave of fangs and claws and dark fists. It was over.

# CHAPTER 18

# UNEXPECTED AID

"**M**onsters, attack!" Herobrine yelled.

The terrifying creatures advanced, their growling voices growing loud with excitement. The Endermen were the first to advance, teleporting right in front of the villagers.

"Remember, look away and don't touch the Endermen!" Gameknight yelled. "Archers, don't accidently shoot one of them. Use your swords instead."

The villagers began to back up, but the sound of monsters behind them filled their ears. The zombies and skeletons that had been entering the tunnel at the center of Dragon's Teeth were now climbing out of the dark opening and heading toward them. Thankfully, they had to go around the lava flow and carefully navigate the flowing streams of water, which slowed them down.

"Smithy, what do we do?" someone asked.

But Gameknight was consumed with fear. He was looking toward the king of the Endermen, his dark red skin bringing back terrifying memories from deep within his soul.

"Smithy . . . help us!" another shouted.

*I don't know what to do,* Gameknight thought.

Erebus turned and stared at him, his red eyes boring into him like two intense lasers. Gameknight glanced away quickly, so as to not enrage the evil creature. He wanted to apologize to all the villagers for bringing them here. He was no leader . . . not like Smithy. He was just a scared kid.

Reaching up, he adjusted his iron helmet. For a moment, Gameknight thought about removing it and exposing himself for the lie that he was, but he knew that would do nothing but make the situation worse.

*I have to think of something, or all these villagers will be killed.*

He looked at Weaver, the young NPC's blue eyes filled with fear. *If he dies here, what would happen to Crafter and my other friends?* His mind was so consumed with thoughts of failure and fear that he couldn't even move.

Zombies began to clash with villagers as skeletons fired their arrows at the intruders. Like the zombies, the ferocity the skeletons and the spiders suddenly possessed was startling. One zombie attacked Gameknight, its long claws slicing and tearing.

This snapped Gameknight into action.

With his two swords a blur, he attacked the creature, slashing at it over and over until it disappeared with a *pop.* Glancing around the battlefield, Gameknight could tell they had no chance. But at least if they were going to fail, they would go down fighting.

Suddenly, music filled the air. It was a soothing sound that seemed to quell the fires of panic in the NPCs, while at the same time driving the monsters into fits of anguish. A loud clap of thunder sounded, filling the air. It was so deafening that it made everyone's ears ring, startling the monsters and making them pull back.

"What was that?" Fencer asked.

Gameknight shrugged. The thunder boomed again, but this time, a bolt of lightning struck the ground like a brilliant dagger of white fire. It created a bright radiant ball of electricity that hovered there for an instant, then faded away. When Gameknight's eyes finally adjusted again, he saw an old woman standing where the lightning had struck. In her hand was a crooked wooden walking stick, the end capped with metal.

She glanced at Gameknight and the other villagers, giving each a reassuring, grandmotherly smile, then turned and glared at Herobrine, pointing at the monster with her cane.

"The end for you, Virus, has just begun," she said in a scratchy voice.

Her hands began to glow a deep forest green that spread up her arms and then her elbows. Before Herobrine could reply, she stooped over and plunged her shimmering hands into the stone ground. Instantly, new creatures began to pop into existence, each looking completely different from the next. There was one wearing a dusty smock, patches of dirt on its sleeves and legs as well as on the creature's hair and face. Another appeared with dark brown skin that looked rough, like wrinkled sand paper. His dark hair stuck out in all directions like a tangle of branches from a bird's nest. More of them appeared all across the battlefield, each one completely unique in appearance.

"Who is that old woman?" one of the villagers asked.

No one answered. They were all in shock as they watched what was happening.

Gameknight999 smiled as he looked at his old friend, the Oracle. He'd been on many adventures with the old woman, battling Herobrine in the future. And now she was bringing her light-crafters here to help.

And then, as if responding to some silent command from the wrinkled woman, the light-crafters moved into action. The dirty one began throwing tiny cubes across the ground. When each one landed, it changed the rocky ground into soil. Another threw what looked like little green missiles at the newly transformed dirt. When they hit, they formed a sapling that sprung into a full-grown tree seconds later. The oaks and spruces formed a barrier between the monsters and the villagers.

"Behind us!" Gameknight shouted.

The newcomers continued to block the monsters from approaching with a line of trees. Zombies tried to move between the trunks, but another creature caused long blades of grass to grow, entangling any monster that stepped too close.

The old woman moved to Gameknight as more of the strange NPCs materialized.

"We must leave this place quickly, child, if all are to survive," the old woman said.

"Who are you?" Carver asked.

"I am the . . ."

"She's the Oracle," Gameknight said, a grateful smile on his face.

The Oracle turned her head toward Gameknight999, her gray hair flinging across her face, then falling down again to her shoulders.

"That is correct," she said suspiciously. "I've been sent to get Minecraft back in balance as well as to deal with that virus. But first, it is time for all of you to head back to your village." She turned and pointed to a couple of the new creatures. "Snowbrin, Icebrin, get on either side and form barriers to keep the monsters back." She then turned to face another group. "Grassbrin, keep the monsters back. Treebrin, Leafbrin, do the same. Light-crafters, we must encourage the monsters to stay away without hurting any of them."

"Who cares if you hurt them?!" Carver exclaimed.

"We are not here to kill," the Oracle said, her voice sounding very grandmotherly and wise. "We are here to repair."

"But—"

She held up a wrinkled hand, silencing the NPC, then turned back to her light-crafters, positioning more of them around the company of NPCs.

"It's time. Let's go."

With a wave of her pale old hand, a line of trees disappeared. Instantly, zombies tried to charge in, but a wall of snow and ice appeared on either side of their escape route, encapsulating the monsters in a temporarily-frozen prison.

"Everyone, this way," she said.

Moving faster than anyone thought possible, the Oracle sprinted through the opening with a group of light-crafters on either side. Grassbrin threw clumps of long, stringy grass at the monsters while Snowbrin and Icebrin formed frosty walls to keep the monsters back. Glancing behind, Gameknight saw Treebrin and Leafbrin creating an impossible tangle of leaves and trees behind them, discouraging any of the monsters from following.

"You were lucky again, blacksmith," Herobrine growled as the party ran away from Dragon's Teeth. "But next time, it'll be you and me on the battlefield, and no old woman will be able to protect you. Your destruction is inevitable!"

"The monsters are leaving," the Oracle said, slowing to a walk. "You have a village nearby, I assume?"

"Yes, we have a desert village," Carver said. "It's on the other side of the Great Chasm."

"Perhaps you should lead us there with great haste," the Oracle said. She winked at Gamenight999 and gave him a slight smile. "I fear there is much preparation needed and little time to accomplish everything necessary. There is little doubt the virus will be enraged by my appearance and double his efforts to destroy everything."

Gameknight nodded as he looked at the Oracle. The last time he'd seen her was at the jungle temple. She'd refused to go with them across the ocean in boats, and had instead stayed behind to slow Herobrine and his monstrous hordes. The evil virus had destroyed her body, but part of her had survived the final encounter. She had still always been present in Minecraft, in Gameknight's time, being the music that resonated across the land. He had just heard that music again, just before her appearance, but for some reason it did not bring him the peace and tranquility that it had in the past. With her appearance here, Gameknight knew that they must be in serious trouble, and that the survival of Minecraft hung in the balance.

## CHAPTER 19

# HEROBRINE'S RAGE

"Who *was* that woman?!" Herobrine shouted, his eyes blazing a harsh white as his rage overflowed. "And what were those creatures she spawned?"

"I think they were a response to your shadow-crafters," Erebus said. "They were probably . . . ahh . . . light-crafters?"

"Light-crafters!?" the Maker exclaimed. "What is going on?!"

Herobrine wanted to destroy something, to vent his rage on some innocent bystander, but he didn't feel like wasting any of his monsters at the moment. Teleporting out into the Overworld, the furious virus found a harmless, innocent cow. Drawing his sword, he attacked the beast, swinging his blade with unbridled fury until the creature disappeared with a *pop*. It happened so quickly, the animal didn't even get a chance to cry out or run. It just simply ceased to exist after Herobrine poured all of his fury onto the poor creature.

With his lust for violence sated just a bit, he teleported back into the huge zombie-town that hid underground beneath Dragon's Teeth.

"Tell me what you saw," Herobrine commanded to the Enderman king.

"The light-crafters seem similar to your shadow-crafters," Erebus began. "Each has a thing that it can craft. One made trees, another made grass, while two of them made snow and ice. Each has a thing they can craft, and we only saw a few of them in that battle. Likely there are many more ready who work for that old woman, just as you have many shadow-crafters working for you. The entrance of the old woman and the light-crafters has evened out the balance of power."

"I don't like things being balanced," Herobrine said as he paced back and forth across the zombie-town. "Not one bit."

He looked up and surveyed the rough-hewn chamber. He could see scores of zombies, skeletons, spiders, and creepers, but he knew more were gathered in all the other zombie-towns across the Overworld. Soon, with the help of his Endermen, Herobrine would bring all those monsters here, to Dragon's Teeth. From here, they would march upon the NPCs and destroy that blacksmith once and for all.

The Maker moved near a stream of lava that flowed out of the ceiling, forming a pool of molten stone on the ground. He breathed in the luscious smoke and ash, the acrid smells calming his rage.

"We need to be prepared for that old woman and her pathetic little crafters," Erebus said.

"Do not fear, my friend," Herobrine said. "When I bring all those monsters here to this zombie-town, we will have such an overwhelming force that those villagers will cower in fear. There are no other villagers nearby, so no reinforcements will be available to the blacksmith, Smithy. But we, however, have many more monsters coming to our aid." He paused to take in a smoky breath. "I just would like to know more about that old hag that appeared before us."

"Well, we know one thing important about her," Erebus said.

"What?" Herobrine snapped.

"She can be destroyed," the king of the Endermen said. "If she was indestructible, then she wouldn't have run away and built barriers to protect herself and her light-crafters. That tells me that she and her minions can, and *will*, be defeated."

"Hmmm . . ." Herobrine mused. "Perhaps you're right."

The Maker turned and glanced at Shaikulud. An evil smile slowly crept across his face as evil thoughts filled his mind.

"Of course I'm right. Now, spider queen, I have something special in mind for you," Herobrine said with a malicious smile. "When it's time, we'll teach the blacksmith a lesson and deal with that woman as well." He turned to face Erebus. "Pass the word: it's time for all my monsters to congregate here. Herobrine's army will be the biggest collection of fangs and claws ever seen!"

He laughed again as his eyes glowed with a harsh, white light that lit the zombie-town as if it were under the noonday sun.

# CHAPTER 20

# MAKING A CHOICE

The NPCs moved quietly through the birch forest, all of them watching nervously for monsters to come charging at them out from behind the trees. In the distance, they could still hear the growls of zombies and the clatter of skeletons, but they did not sound as if they were in pursuit. Likely, the presence of their saviors had worried Herobrine, and he was choosing to be cautious instead of careless.

"So who are you, exactly?" Carver asked the old woman as he moved up to her side.

"As I said earlier, I am the Oracle," she said, as if that explanation would have any meaning to the NPCs.

Carver looked at Fencer, confused, then shrugged his shoulders and moved back to help one of the injured villagers. The Oracle took stock of the light-crafters around her, making sure they were watching the forest with keen eyes. She then moved to Gameknight's side.

"How did you know who I was?" the Oracle asked in a low voice.

"Well . . . that's a difficult question to answer," he whispered.

"You're different than the rest," the old woman said. "I can see letters above your head. They spell out your name, right?"

Gameknight was shocked. "You can see them?"

The Oracle nodded.

"But the other NPCs cannot see them, can they?" he asked.

She shook her head.

"They call me Smithy," Gameknight said. "Please don't use the other name, the one you can see over my head. The villagers wouldn't understand."

"So you're posing as this Smithy?" she asked.

Gameknight hesitated. He glanced around, to make sure the villagers were far enough away, then lowered his voice just to be safe. "Yes. Smithy was their leader. I took on his guise when Smithy was killed, to keep the villagers working together. It's important that they continue to think of me as Smithy."

"I can tell you don't seem very happy about this ruse," the Oracle said in a whisper.

Gameknight sighed. "Smithy was a great leader. He cared about his villagers and would do nothing to put them into danger. Meanwhile I just led them into a trap and nearly got them all killed. I'm no Smithy."

Gameknight hung his head down and watched his feet as he trudged through the forest.

"So you doubt your ability to lead these NPCs to safety?" she asked.

Gameknight sighed again and nodded his head. "I'm afraid I'm going to lead them into disaster."

"But you led them out into the desert and defeated the zombie king," she said.

Gameknight stared at the old woman. "How did you know about that?" he asked. "You weren't there."

"When I was programmed, I was given the history of what has transpired in Minecraft," the Oracle replied.

"Programmed? What do you mean?" Gameknight asked. "Who programmed you?"

"You know who," she said as she pointed up into the sky with a bent and wrinkled finger.

"Notch?" the User-that-is-not-a-user asked after a moment.

She nodded her head.

"He sensed Minecraft getting out of balance and detected the virus that is Herobrine. I am—"

"You're the *anti*virus," Gameknight said.

"Correct. I have been sent into Minecraft to put everything back the way it should be. The light-crafters around us are here to counteract the damage being done by Herobrine's shadow-crafters."

Gameknight nodded his head.

"I understand, but how are we going to stop Herobrine?" the User-that-is-not-a-user asked. "He had a lot of monsters back there and probably even more underground. We don't have anywhere near enough villagers to fight off that many."

"Matching sword for claws is not the way to defeat this host of monsters," the Oracle said. "What's needed is true leadership and courage to overcome the destructive force being assembled by Herobrine."

Gameknight hung his head down again, as thoughts of uncertainty and fear filled his mind.

"I don't know if I can do it, Oracle," he whispered as he looked up into her steel-gray eyes. "I'm not Smithy. Sometimes I feel as if I should just tell them, but then I'm afraid they'll feel betrayed and turn on me. The villagers will think I've been lying to them all this time and will never trust me again. I couldn't bear that. It's in my nature to help, but I feel as if I'm doing more harm than good." He hung his head down again, feeling like he wanted to just disappear.

"Deep down inside, we all know there are limits to our strengths and it can feel like there is great depth to our weaknesses," the Oracle explained. "But sometimes, those boundaries can shift, for strengths and weaknesses are only choices that we make within ourselves. You can choose to ignore your weaknesses and just focus on your strengths, if you have the courage. All you need is to believe."

"Believe?" Gameknight asked.

He looked up at her and thought he saw her eyes sparkle just bit, like the way Crafter's did when he was giving Gameknight one of his many lessons of wisdom.

"Yes, believe," she continued. "You can choose to believe you're a great leader, and if you truly believe it, then it will be so. But if you doubt yourself and focus on your weaknesses, then everyone around you will sense that, and your leadership will crumble. It comes down to a simple choice: do you believe in yourself or not?"

*Do I believe in myself?* Gameknight thought. *What kind of question is that?*

He'd fought countless battles all across Minecraft, faced the four horsemen of the apocalypse created by Herobrine, faced the spider queen, faced Malacoda, faced Erebus, and even faced Herobrine himself multiple times. But the fact was, he'd been terrified every time, and just narrowly avoided defeat by using some kind of trick, like pigs or water or iron golems or TNT.

The puzzle pieces began to tumble around in his head at the thought of the explosive cubes. TNT was somehow part of the solution to the problem he faced, but he wasn't even sure he knew what the problem was.

Gameknight knew if he didn't come up with a brilliant solution, then Herobrine would likely kill the ancestors of his friends. If that happened, then Crafter, Hunter, Stitcher, Digger, and Herder would never be born. The thought filled him with jagged slivers of fear, and as his anxiety grew, the puzzle pieces disappeared, fading into the uncertainty and dread filling his soul.

But then, a memory surfaced from within his mind. It was when he and Stitcher and Herder had saved Hunter from the clutches of Malacoda's monsters. A group of wither skeletons had imprisoned Hunter in an iron cage. He and his friends were completely outnumbered, yet the scrawny Herder had figured out what to do. Without the slightest trace of fear, the lanky boy had gathered a pack of wolves and used them to attack the skeletons. The young boy, who many thought was a useless coward, had just acted, taking advantage of what he did best to help his friends. Gameknight smiled when he remembered the look of joy on Hunter's face when they saved her.

The image slowly faded from his mind, only to be replaced by another. It was of Crafter at the Alamo. Erebus had been chasing them across the Overworld, looking to destroy enough NPCs to move up to the next server plane, in hopes of reaching the Source. Gameknight and Crafter had lured the monsters into a huge cave filled with users and a trap designed by his friend, Shawny. But the trap had failed. Endermen had disabled the redstone before they could trigger the trap and destroy all the monsters. Crafter had acted without thinking, running into the midst of the monster army so he could trigger the redstone manually, blowing up monsters's escape route and himself at the same time, trapping the monsters in the cavern. The aged NPC didn't even think about the consequences nor did he think *what if* . . . he just reacted and did what he did best, and that was helping his friends.

Thoughts about Digger saving his life in a stronghold library next surfaced in his mind, along with the countless times that Hunter and Stitcher had saved him and others with their bows. His mind was soon filled with countless memories of NPCs doing the extraordinary to help someone else. Gameknight was humbled to have known them and fought at their side.

But then he realized that one thing linked all of these instances in time: the User-that-is-not-a-user. He had brought these NPCs together. His strength and confidence had drawn out the best in them, and without Gameknight999, they would likely have never become friends. He'd been the glue that had kept the band of friends together when everything seemed hopeless. He'd been the reason to keep on trying. He knew now that giving up only guaranteed the outcome, while trying meant there was still hope.

Glue . . . still hope . . . maybe there was more to him than just the helmet that hid his face. Maybe he could lead these people, but not by doing what he thought Smithy might do. Instead, he had to do what Gameknight999, the king of the griefers, would do.

He glanced at Fencer and adjusted his iron helmet. The NPC gave him a worried look, as if he thought Gameknight was going to remove the helmet and come clean. But Gameknight knew he couldn't do that now; the presence of Smithy was a big part of the glue holding this army together, and he had to continue to play his part for their sake. But he was done trying to be Smithy. He would keep this disguise on, but it was time for Gameknight999 to take command and do things that only the User-that-is-not-a-user would dare. It was time to stop *worrying* and start *doing.* And in that instant, a wave of confidence filled him as tiny square goose bumps covered his arms.

Turning to the Oracle, he found the old woman had a smile on her face, her gray eyes sparkling with optimism. She did not say a word; she just nodded her head, somehow knowing what was going on within him.

*I* do *believe,* Gameknight thought.

The puzzle pieces began to tumble around within his head once again. There was a solution to the problem of Herobrine and his monster army; he just needed to be patient and find it. While he searched, he'd prepare his pieces on the game board at the same time that Herobrine prepared his. Soon, he'd teach that evil virus what it was like to battle with an experienced user.

"We need to get back to the village quickly," Gameknight said suddenly, in a loud, clear voice. "There are many preparations to be made, and little time to do it."

"We're almost to the bridge," Carver exclaimed. "We'll be back to the village before dusk."

"Let's hurry," Weaver said.

"Oink," the pig added.

Some of the villagers laughed.

The young boy began to run, still clutching the nervous Wilbur in his arms. When he reached Gameknight999, the User-that-is-not-a-user ran with him, casting a confident smile toward the old woman.

# CHAPTER 21

# BACK TO THE VILLAGE

"There it is!" Carver exclaimed.

When Gameknight crested the sand dune, he saw what the stocky NPC was pointing at: the desert village. Thick walls of cobblestone stood high around the perimeter of the community, rocky crenellations dotting the top. Tall, cylindrical towers sat on each corner stretching high up into the air. At the center of the village, a watchtower loomed high into the sky, extending up maybe thirty blocks and giving the watcher that stood at the top a clear view of the surrounding landscape in all directions. Torches burned brightly along the wall and on all the towers, and warriors stood proud on the battlements, iron swords glistening in the light.

Gameknight could see archers standing atop the towers and watchers in the central cobblestone tower. They all held bows in their hands with arrows notched, ready to be fired. The sharp projectiles were all pointed out into the desert as they cautiously watched the party approach.

The sun was sinking near the horizon, casting a pale red light on the sandy desert. To the east, the sky was already black, the sparkling faces of the stars emerging from the fading blue sky.

"Carver, I think it might be wise to pull out a torch and show them who we are," Gameknight said.

"Yeah, you're probably right," he replied.

Reaching into his inventory, he pulled out a torch, which magically lit as he held it aloft, casting a circle of warm, yellow light around the party.

"Weaver, go to the back of the group and pull out a torch," Gameknight said. "We don't want anyone shooting at us accidently." The young NPC set Wilbur on the ground and ran to the rear of the procession. He pulled out a torch, casting more light on the back of the formation.

"Oink," the pig said, glad to be able to stretch his tiny legs again.

"It's our villagers!" one of the NPCs shouted from the cobblestone watchtower.

Slowly, the archers lowered their bows as a pair of iron doors creaked open in the fortified wall, allowing the weary travels to enter. Carver was the first to move into the village, running forward to find his parents and brother, Baker.

When Gameknight finally passed through the doors, whispers and comments spread through the community.

"It's him!"

"It's Smithy . . ."

"Smithy of the Two-Swords . . ."

Villagers looked at him with awe as he entered, many of them reaching out to touch him lightly on the arm or shoulder. Gameknight was moved at their confidence in him, but even more, he was shocked at how many NPCs were behind the forti-fied walls. There were hundreds of people, from all different walks of life, each with a common purpose: to help Smithy stop the evil plans of Herobrine.

"Where did all these people come from?" Gameknight asked one of the villagers.

"The runners that you sent out found village after village," one of the NPCs explained.

Looking at his smock and the tiny cuts all along his hands and arms, Gameknight could tell he was a digger.

"They started arriving just after you left," Digger explained. "More are expected before dawn, and even more after that. We're having them hide down in the crafting chamber away from the prying eyes of monsters, but when they heard you had returned, they all came up to greet the famous Smithy of the Two-Swords."

Gameknight was humbled. These people were putting their lives in his hands, and he refused to let them down. He thought about removing his hel-met and telling the truth, but Smithy was the glue that would hold this group of individuals together into a cohesive fighting force, and he needed to respect that.

Once everyone had entered the village and the gates had closed, the NPCs noticed the Oracle and light-crafters. Gameknight held out his hands and motioned all the villagers on the walls and towers to come down and hear what he had to say.

"This is our new friend, the Oracle, and these are her light-crafters," Gameknight said in a loud voice. "They are here to help us in this war with Herobrine. Someone show the light-crafters to the crafting chamber. I'm sure they have work they need to do. Everyone else, welcome our new friends, then get back to work. Tunnels need to still be dug to the other villages, and we need more armor and weapons. We must be prepared when it's time to meet Herobrine and his army of monsters."

"SMITHY!" the villagers shouted, then went to work.

He glanced at the Oracle, and she gave him a nod. The light-crafters were then led off to the crafting chamber. The old woman moved next to Gameknight and pulled him away from the crowd. Fencer noticed and headed toward them. She glanced at Fencer suspiciously as he moved to the User-that-is-not-a-user's side.

Gameknight nodded. "He knows."

She nodded in return. "I see you are continuing to wear your Smithy mask," she said softly.

"It's likely best for now," the User-that-is-not-a-user replied.

"Just because you are posing as someone else, that doesn't mean you can't be you," the Oracle added.

"I know. I came to the same conclusion," Gameknight replied. "What will you have the light-crafters do first?"

"Treebrin, Dirtbrin, Cactusbrin, and Grassbrin are outside, improving the defenses around the village," she explained.

"Why do their names all end in 'brin'?" Fencer asked.

"All light-crafters' names end with 'brin,' and the shadow-crafters' names end in 'brine.' I don't really know why it's that way. That's just how they were all programmed."

She walked toward the village's well and spoke in a loud voice so that others could hear.

"My light-crafters will be busy in your crafting chamber," she explained. "I've instructed Armorbrin to get to work on something special for all of you, as well as Swordbrin and the other tool light-crafters. You may want to start collecting more iron; I suspect you'll need it very soon."

Gameknight pointed at Digger. The big NPC nodded and collected a group of stocky villagers. With their pickaxes over their shoulder, they headed for the watchtower and the secret tunnel that led to the crafting chamber and the village's mines.

Suddenly, the desert came alive with the sound of clicking, as if a million crickets had surrounded the community. Moving faster than Gameknight thought was possible, the Oracle dashed to Fencer and whispered into his ear. The NPC listened carefully, then nodded his head and took off running for the crafting chamber.

"Everyone, to the walls!" someone shouted, but Gameknight could tell by the sounds that it was already too late for that.

"NO!" he yelled. "Everyone gather around the well. Stand shoulder-to-shoulder and guard those around you. Draw your swords and get ready. Some of you, get on top of the well and get ready to shoot."

The User-that-is-not-a-user spoke with such confidence that the NPCs instantly responded, doing exactly what he said. Some of them glanced at Gameknight, clearly afraid, but by now he had drawn his two swords and had them out for all to see. When they saw the dual blades, the villagers stood a little taller, a little bit of their fear evaporating away. Even though they had no idea how many monsters were attacking, his strong, commanding voice made them feel at ease and ready for this challenge. It surprised Gameknight—not that the villagers were listening to him, but that he felt so confident in this role. He could still play his part as Smithy, for now, but he would do things like Gameknight999, the User-that-is-not-a-user.

Glancing over his shoulder, he saw the Oracle standing inside the circle of swords and found her giving him a self-satisfied smile, as if she could somehow see inside his mind. Gameknight gave her a wink, then stepped forward in front of the defenders, his two swords held at the ready.

"Outside are a bunch of pesky spiders that need to be exterminated," Gameknight said in a loud, confident voice, "and we are the boot that will squash them!"

The NPCs laughed, their chuckles echoing off the stone walls.

"Now everyone, get ready," Gameknight shouted. "Watch out for your neighbors and fight as a team, instead of individuals. We can get through this if we work together."

He turned and faced the gray cobblestone walls. Gripping his swords tightly, he waited for the fuzzy black wave of claws that was about to crash down upon them.

# CHAPTER 22
# MORE SPIDERS

Suddenly, a dark wave crested the top of the fortified wall. The fuzzy black bodies seemed to merge with the darkening sky, their blazing red eyes standing out bright. They moved across the battlements like a black stain spreading across a wall, razor-sharp claws clicking on the stone. The torches along the top of the wall made the monsters easy to see as they made their way along the battlements, spreading out into a long, hateful line. Clearly, they wanted to attack the NPCs from all sides. Fortunately, it was exactly what Gameknight expected them to do.

The spiders climbed the walls without difficulty, coming down the other side and spreading out across the sandy courtyard. They stayed near the walls, hesitant to move forward until given the command. Their mandibles clicked together in a blur, eager to attack.

One of the spiders stayed perched atop the fortified wall rather than joining her sisters on the ground. This lone spider was larger than the rest and boasted bright, purple eyes. Gameknight instantly knew who it was . . . Shaikulud, the spider queen.

"Why don't you come down here, Shaikulud, and face me?" the User-that-is-not-a-user challenged.

"I am not here for you, blackssssmith," the spider queen replied. "I am here for *her*." The monster pointed a dark, curved claw toward the Oracle. "Give her to ussss and we will ssssspare your village."

"You'll have to go through all of us first," Gameknight replied. "The Oracle is under my protection, and I won't let any of your bugs touch her."

"How quickly you have forgotten our lasssst meeting," Shaikulud hissed. "Herobrine hassss been making ssssome improvementsssss on my ssssspidersssss. Ready . . . attack!"

The dark monsters charged forward, but as they neared, something strange happened. The villagers' swords began to glow a faint green. Gameknight instantly felt his blades getting warmer in his hand, as if they were being charged with energy. He looked around and saw the villagers glowing with the same green hue as well. Many of them stood up taller as they, too, were filled with the same glowing power.

Turning, Gameknight glanced at the Oracle and saw a big, knowing grin on her face.

"The light-crafters are helping us now," Gameknight said in a loud voice. "Villagerbrin and Swordbrin just gave us a little assistance."

The old woman nodded her head, her smile growing bigger.

He turned back to the spider queen and saw a look of doubt on her evil face, then cast her a grin.

"Everyone . . . ATTACK!" Gameknight shouted, then ran forward.

All of the villagers followed his lead and charged forward, directly at the spider horde. They swung their swords with greater strength as their weapons did more damage to the eight-legged monsters. Spider claws clashed with iron blades as the two opponents met. Screams of pain came from both villagers and spiders as sharp blades and pointed claws found flesh.

Gameknight slashed at the spider before him, blocking one claw with his left blade as he attacked with his right. He landed a devastating hit, causing the monster to flash red, taking damage. He then slashed at it again and again, blocking clawed attacks while quickly countering with another strike. The monster quickly fell before him, only to be replaced by another one.

Next to him, he saw a woodcutter struggling with his opponent. Gameknight slashed at the monster, drawing its attention to him, which allowed the villager to quickly finish it off.

"Fight together, in pairs!" Gameknight shouted.

He lent his blade to the NPC on his other side, hitting the villager's opponent with all his strength. The monster screeched in pain and tried to move back, but something kept the spider from retreating. Gameknight hit the monster again, finishing it off.

But against the NPCs' improved strength and better swords, the spiders fought viciously, as if retreat was not possible. Gameknight knew that the spider queen controlled all the monsters with her evil mind and would likely not let any of the fuzzy creatures back down. He had to somehow get to her so he could end this battle. But there was no way for him to reach the village walls; he was completely blocked off by spiders.

Suddenly, the sound of boots on gravel came to his ears. Stepping back, Gameknight saw some of the NPCs that had been working in the crafting chamber running out of the cobblestone watchtower. They stopped a dozen blocks away and pulled out bows. Firing at the monsters, they whittled down the monsters' HP and slowly opened a section in the spider line. With their bows singing, they fired on more of the hateful creatures, attacking those at the rear while the swordsmen slashed at the front ranks.

"Attack the queen!" Gameknight shouted. "All archers, fire at the queen on the wall!"

As one, the arrows were turned from the dark monsters to where Shaikulud perched on the fortified wall. They fired a wave of arrows that streaked through the air like pointed lightning. The arrows sparkled with a green glow as Arrowbrin, in the crafting chamber underground, added his contribution to the battle.

Shaikulud had no choice but to jump from the wall to escape certain death. In that moment, her psychic hold over the spiders wavered, allowing the monsters to choose their lives over their courage; they retreated. The fuzzy giants turned and ran for the walls of the village, but the archers did not let them get very far. They drove their shafts into the monsters as fast as they could draw arrows and release. Many of the dark creatures fell under the pointed hail, but many also escaped.

As the spiders ran from the village and disappeared into the desert, the villagers took to the walls again and yelled insults at the fading monsters. Gameknight stared out into the evening landscape and watched them get swallowed up by the surrounding night.

"Shaikulud, tell Herobrine that we're still here!" Gameknight shouted. "Tell him, if he wants to face Smithy, I'll be here waiting for him! Tell that viral coward that Smithy of the Two-Swords is not afraid!"

The villagers cheered and patted Gameknight999 on the back, many of them saying, "Smithy be crazy." And for the briefest of moments, he actually did feel like Smithy of the Two-Swords.

*Maybe I can lead them to victory*, Gameknight thought.

Glancing back to the well, he saw the Oracle standing there, nodding her head, a huge smile stretching across her square face.

# CHAPTER 23

# SPIES

Gameknight sighed as he listened to the moans and cries that filled the village. Many NPCs were wounded and in dire need of healing, but many had also been killed. Family members mourned those they lost, while friends tried to console the grieving villagers. It was a sad thing to watch, and the User-that-is-not-a-user felt guilty for not having saved more of them.

"It could have been much worse," a scratchy voice said next to him in consolation.

Gameknight turned to face the Oracle, her wooden cane tapping its metal tip on the sandstone ground.

"Your leadership and courage kept the villagers working together," she pointed out. "And as you know, that's the only way to defeat Herobrine's monsters—by working together."

"I know," Gameknight replied. "I'm still sad that so many had to perish in that battle, but I know that I did everything I could do to save everyone. It's just . . ."

"Just what?" the old woman asked.

"It's just that Herobrine had his spiders attack just out of spite, to make us suffer," he growled. "He knew we would never just turn you over to the spiders. This attack wasn't some strategic move to gain land or capture critical resources. He just wanted us to feel pain, for no reason other than it would please him."

"That is the nature of a virus," the Oracle said in a scratchy voice. "Its only purpose is to spread out as far as it can, then do as much damage as possible. That is what Herobrine wants to do. First, he will try to reach out across this server, then he'll try to get to the other servers in the pyramid of servers until he has destroyed everything."

"I'm not gonna allow that," the User-that-is-not-a-user said with a scowl.

"I know, child," she replied.

Glancing up to the square moon high overhead, Gameknight could see a thick layer of clouds arriving, the sparkling stars slowly being swallowed up by the boxy veil. The feline cries of the ghasts could be heard as the clouds drew closer. The Oracle heard the sounds and smiled.

"Those are ghasts up there," Gameknight said. "Why do you smile?"

"They are like floating children," the Oracle said. "Their only desire is to float in the sky and drag their tentacles through the thick clouds. They are completely harmless and a beautiful feature in Minecraft."

"In my time, they are horrible monsters that would kill us all if they saw us down here," Gameknight said. "I don't know why they are so docile in this time, but I don't trust them and never will."

"You have much hatred in your heart," the Oracle said.

"I have been through a lot and seen a lot of suffering," Gameknight said. "And Herobrine has been at the center of it all. He must be stopped."

"Well, that's why I'm here," she replied, then cupped her hands over her ears.

Gameknight gave her a confused look, but she only smiled back. Suddenly, thunder growled overhead and a bolt of lightning flashed across the sky, striking the ground far from the desert village.

"You knew that was going to happen," Gameknight said, his eyes wide.

The Oracle nodded. "It was my doing," she said. "I make the lightning strike the ground when something in Minecraft must be reset . . . in this case, it was lava. One of Herobrine's shadow-crafters has been making lava hotter, and it is putting things out of balance. We can't have that."

"So that lightning fixes that?" Gameknight asked.

The old woman nodded, her gray eyes sparkling with satisfaction.

"I wait until the shadow-crafters are not ready, then I make the lightning strike," the Oracle said. "Lavabrine was not paying attention, so I reset some of his work."

"Nice," Gameknight replied with a smile.

Suddenly, Watcher yelled out from the top of the cobblestone watchtower. "Something's coming!"

Gameknight ran to the steps that led to the top of the fortified wall. He peered out into the desert and could just barely see movement in the darkness.

"Archers, get ready," Fencer said. "But don't fire until you see what you're shooting at."

Newly strengthened bows, improved by the light-crafters, creaked as arrows and strings were drawn back. Gameknight took out his own bow and aimed at the shapes moving about in the desert. The clouds had completely covered the moon, plunging the landscape into almost complete darkness, with only the torches on the walls casting any illumination onto the sands.

"Who's out there?" Gameknight shouted. "We have five hundred arrows aimed at you right now. Identify yourself!"

"Five hundred arrows?" Fencer asked at his side.

"Well, I sorta exaggerated a bit," he said with a smile.

Fencer slapped him on the back and laughed.

"Don't shoot," a voice called back.

Suddenly, a torch flared to life, revealing a huge group of NPCs approaching the village. Gameknight was shocked. There must have been sixty or seventy villagers trudging across the sand dunes. They looked exhausted.

"Open the gates," the User-that-is-not-a-user shouted quickly. "Everyone, put down your bows. They're friends."

The archers lowered their weapons and cheered as their fellow NPCs entered the village. Many of the warriors ran down the steps to greet the newcomers, while others stayed on the walls, peering out into the shadowy desert, watching for monsters.

"This brings our numbers up to more than three hundred now," Fencer said. "You can be sure Herobrine will be surprised when he sees all our warriors."

"Perhaps, but I'm sure he has monsters posted close by to see what we are doing," Gameknight said. "We should send out patrols to watch the desert around the village. We should also place some torches out there so we can see the landscape better at night."

Fencer glanced at a group of warriors that had been listening and gave them a nod. They gathered their weapons and armor, and headed for the gates, torches in hand.

"Groups of warriors will keep patrolling all night long," Fencer said.

"No one goes alone," the User-that-is-not-a-user insisted.

Fencer nodded and gave more instructions to some warriors, then turned back to Gameknight999.

"You look nervous," the NPC said.

"I was just thinking, we really don't know what Herobrine is doing or how many monsters he really has," Gameknight replied. "All we saw were the ones that attacked us back at Dragon's Teeth. We really don't know what's going on there."

"Let's call all the village elders together and discuss this," Fencer suggested.

Gameknight nodded, then moved toward the village well. Soon, all of the oldest and wisest villagers approached, worried looks on their faces.

"Smithy has asked for this gathering," Fencer said after all the necessary NPCs had arrived. "He has some concerns."

Some of the villagers murmured to each other, speculating what this was about, but when Gameknight stepped forward, they all grew silent and turned their square heads toward him.

"We need more information," he said. "We have no idea what Herobrine's doing, or how many monsters he has, which kinds, and what they are training for. Without better intelligence, we're blind and will likely just stumble into a trap like we did at Dragon's Teeth."

"Maybe we can just wait here and force him to come to us," Baker, Carver's older brother suggested. "That way we can fight him on our own ground and on our own terms."

"No, we'll be trapped here behind our walls," Carver said.

Many of the elders glared at Carver, as if his comments were inappropriate and unwelcome. The big NPC lowered his gaze to the ground and took a step back, as though he wasn't important enough to be a part of the discussion.

"No, Carver is right!" Gameknight said. He turned his head toward the stocky NPC and cast him a smile. "Mobility is key in warfare; moving targets are harder to hit. If we stay here, behind our walls, then we're forced to wait until Herobrine figures out a way to defeat us. He could just choose to wait until we all starve, though it's unlikely Herobrine would do that. He doesn't care how many of his monsters die in his conquest to dominate the Overworld. All he wants is for everyone to suffer. We need to stay one step ahead of him, if we're gonna have any chance of defeating him."

"But how do we do that?" Farmer asked.

"We send out some spies," Weaver said.

Everyone turned toward the young voice. Slowly, Weaver stepped out of the shadows, wearing leather armor that had been dyed black.

"This is a meeting for the elders, not kids," one of the older NPCs chided. "And where did you get that ridiculous armor?"

Weaver ignored the question and continued to speak.

"What will be decided here affects all of us, even the kids that have been fighting right alongside all of you. So we should all have a voice too."

"He makes a good point," Fencer said, nodding his head.

"OK, Weaver, so what do you suggest?" Gameknight asked.

"Have Tanner make leather armor for a small group of warriors, but have him dye them all black, like what I'm wearing now. Then they can go out at night and spy on monsters. Send them out in groups of four. When they learn something, send a pair of them back with the information. No one is ever alone, as they're always in pairs. And by hiding in the shadows, we can learn what the monsters are doing, and how many troops they really have."

Gameknight glanced around at the collection of NPCs. Many of them were nodding their heads as they considered the idea.

"It's a good idea," one of the elders acquiesced, though he still cast Weaver an angry scowl.

"I agree," said another.

Gameknight looked around the group and found all of them nodding their heads.

"OK, then we will do as Weaver suggests," the User-that-is-not-a-user said. "We'll get Tanner working on armor right away."

"I already took the liberty of getting him started," Weaver added with a smile.

"You did, huh?" Gameknight replied. "Very well, we'll send out the fastest runners, in groups of four, to Dragon's Teeth. When we know what is going on, we'll formulate a battle plan."

"Great!" Weaver exclaimed.

"Don't get too excited, Weaver, because you aren't going. You'll be staying here, helping me plan our defense in case Herobrine decides to attack us here."

"But . . ."

"We must all do our part, and that is yours," Gameknight said firmly.

The young boy could tell from the tone of his voice that resistance was futile, so he simply nodded at the blacksmith. With everyone in agreement, the meeting adjourned.

Gameknight walked up to the top of the fortified wall and stared out onto the desert. He could see new trees standing tall around the village with hundreds of cactuses placed all over, making a frontal assault difficult; Treebrin and Cactusbrin had been busy. As they discussed the defenses, Gameknight heard the village gates open, and a dozen shadowy villagers slipped out into the desert. They looked like black shadows as they sprinted across the dunes, and, in seconds, they disappeared into the dark landscape, all of them heading toward Dragon's Teeth and certain danger.

## CHAPTER 24

# CREEPER ARMY

A deep, blood-red light filled the eastern horizon as the sun peered over the distant mountains. Herobrine loved that single moment every day, when the skyline turned that specific shade of red. It lasted for only a few seconds, but it was his favorite time of day. The yellow face of the sun rose a little higher, changing the blood red to a bright crimson that quickly faded to orange. Herobrine sighed. The moment was gone, and now lousy morning was upon them.

The dark sky to the west, with the last remnants of a star-filled sky, slowly faded to a deep, clear, disgusting blue. The clouds that had blocked the moon and most of the stars through the evening had continued to move westward and were now far away. Herobrine had heard thunder and saw brief flashes of light in the middle of the night. It had happened far to the west, out in the desert, but now all was quiet as the clear blue sky dominated the heavens.

Turning his attention from the awful blue sky, Herobrine watched as monsters from all over the Overworld continued to arrive. Throughout the night, the flow of monsters had been huge, but now it was but a trickle. He had drained the biomes adjacent to the extreme hills where Dragon's Teeth was located of all their monsters and had sent emissaries to those farther out. The only creatures left to collect were those in the other zombie-towns hidden throughout the Overworld. Soon he would call them all and then they would move against the blacksmith and his puny villagers.

Beneath him, the monsters that hid underground in the massive zombie-town felt confused. Somehow, he could feel their thoughts and emotions with his evil artificial-intelligence virus software. It was as if he were slightly connected to every nearby monster, his viral tendrils intertwined with the fabric of Minecraft.

The monsters in the massive chamber had no idea why they were there, and many were scared. But Herobrine didn't care. Monsters were all disposable, and if they were unhappy or scared, who cared? All that mattered was their obedience.

Suddenly, the presence of a massive group of monsters appeared in his mind. It felt like a tidal wave of creatures slowly flowing across the landscape. They were approaching from the east, moving quietly through the forest.

Turning, Herobrine spotted them. They appeared like a flowing, mottled green-and-black carpet. The huge army of creepers moved through the forest in complete silence, their tiny little feet moving in a blur. He could see a small number of the creepers with blue sparks running along their skin, like a suit of sapphire lightning. These were clearly charged creepers, and probably were some of the creeper king's generals.

At the head of the procession, a monster sparkled like the charged creepers, but with the addition of jagged bolts of red power mixed in with the blue electricity. The combination of the red and blue gave off a flickering purple light that lit the forest with a lavender glow.

Gathering his teleportation powers, the Maker disappeared from the peak and materialized next to the flickering monster.

"Oxus, you have returned," Herobrine said to the king of the creepers.

"Yes, Sire," Oxus said. "And I have brought with me enough creepers to stop this war. There are hundreds and hundreds of creepers following me now. The sight of them will force the villagers to negotiate a peace, and give monsters a place in the Overworld without violence."

"Yes, you did very well," Herobrine said, a devious smile on his square face.

Suddenly, Erebus appeared in a cloud of purple mist at the Maker's side.

"Erebus, behold the fabulous gift Oxus brings to us," Herobrine said.

The king of the Endermen glanced at the massive body of creepers marching past, heading for the flat, rocky clearing between the four mountains that made up Dragon's Teeth.

"This many creepers will allow us to—"

Herobrine held up a hand, stopping the Enderman from talking.

"Oxus, take your creepers to the mountain with lava running down its side. On the back side of the mountain, you will find a huge cave. Take your creepers there and keep them quiet. There is a small chamber in the mountain with the waterfall; that will be your quarters. Wait there until I have need of you. Do you understand?"

"Yes, Maker," the creeper king replied, then led his troops toward the lava flow.

As they moved away, Erebus edged closer to Herobrine.

"Maker, that many creepers could devastate the villagers in battle," the Enderman king said, his eyes flaring bright red with excitement.

"Of course, I know that already, Enderman," Herobrine snapped. "I have a plan for how our creeper brothers and sisters will be the most effective." He paced back and forth as his eyes glowed bright white with evil thoughts. "I know the blacksmith will not stay in his village. He will come out and meet us in the desert. I think he will come north, to the top of the Great Chasm. While we have him engaged in battle, the creepers will then go across the bridge that spans the Chasm and sneak in behind them. I will order the creepers to mix in among the villagers, then we will detonate all of them in one massive explosion that will destroy every villager."

Herobrine's eyes glowed brighter as the image of all those villagers being destroyed filled his mind. He stopped pacing and turned to face the Endermen king.

"Hopefully, the blacksmith will survive so that I can face him directly. The spider queen said he has challenged me to battle. Well, I'll accommodate him, but only after I destroy all his friends right in front of him. And when he is overcome with grief, I will fall upon him and make that Smithy beg for mercy . . . only *then* will I destroy him. Nothing can stop us from certain victory!"

Erebus's eyes grew even brighter, the red light splashing on the forest floor like stains of blood.

"Soon, the Overworld will belong to me," the Maker said, "and there's nothing that blacksmith can do about it!"

The king of the Enderman gave off a screechy cackle as he laughed with malicious glee.

# CHAPTER 25

# NEWS

Gameknight waited nervously atop the tower. He knew those brave villagers were doing something incredibly dangerous, staring into the mouth of the beast and expecting they could return unscathed. He desperately hoped their stealthy black armor would protect them; he didn't want more NPCs suffering because of his decisions. But deep down inside, he knew this was the right thing to do.

He stood watch for hours, waiting for news. Fencer tried to get him to come down to eat, but Gameknight refused. Instead, food was brought up to him: bowls of mushroom stew and loaves of bread.

Gameknight watched the desert all night long. He stood at the top of the watchtower during the lightning storm, bolts of electricity striking the desert and flashing in the biomes far away. Clearly, the Oracle must have been resetting a lot of things. He looked down at the center of the village. The Oracle stood next to the well with her arms in her sleeves, completely motionless. Whenever lightning would strike, she would twitch ever so slightly, then go back to her motionless state.

The User-that-is-not-a-user stood watch all night long, while the moon slowly crept toward the western horizon and the clouds cleared in the dawn sky. Then the sun slowly rose, painting a bright red stripe across the horizon; it was now morning.

"Smithy, come down from there," someone shouted from the ground. "There is something you need to see."

Nervous excitement pulsed through his veins like electricity. *They're back . . . already?* Gameknight thought.

Stepping to the ladder, he slid down to the ground floor. Dashing out of the cobblestone structure, he found a group of NPCs standing around the village's armorer, Fencer, who was wearing a proud smile.

"What is it?" Gameknight asked.

"We have something new," Fencer said as he patted the craftsman on the back.

"What are you talking about?" he asked.

"Show him," Fencer said.

The NPC reached into his inventory and pulled out a bright sword that glowed a translucent blue, as if it were carved from glacial ice. He offered it to Gameknight, hilt first. When the morning sun hit the razor-sharp blade, it gleamed as if alive with some kind of internal cerulean flame. Gameknight took it in his hand and gripped the handle firmly. As he held it high in the air, a huge smile stretched across his face. Pulling his iron sword from his inventory with his left hand, he held the two weapons high in the sky. The villagers cheered and banged their weapons against their leather armor, making a rhythmical thud that echoed through the village.

"How is this possible?" Gameknight asked.

"Swordbrin has been busy in the crafting chamber," Armorer replied.

"This is fantastic," the User-that-is-not-a-user exclaimed as he put away his weapons.

"There's more," Fencer said with a devious grin.

Armorer stepped forward and presented a handful of dull gray metal to Gameknight999. Reaching out, he took the items, confused, then recognized what they were.

"Iron armor . . . nice," the User-that-is-not-a-user said.

"Put it on," Armorer said.

Gameknight smiled at him and reached up to remove his leather tunic, but suddenly he remembered that he was wearing Smithy's dark leather armor. Underneath was Gameknight's normal blue shirt and green pants. He couldn't show that to the villagers; they'd instantly recognize him as an imposter.

"How is this possible?" the User-that-is-not-a-user asked.

"The light-crafter, Armorbrin, made a few changes to what we could craft," Fencer said. "Now we can make iron chest plates, leggings and boots. Finally, you have a complete set of armor to go with your iron helmet."

Gameknight wrapped his blocky knuckles against the hard metal, thinking. They made a dull thudding sound.

"This is fantastic!" he exclaimed. "I am truly grateful for this wonderful gift. But if I am to wield this fabulous diamond sword, I think someone else should wear the iron armor."

He scanned the crowd, then found his target. He knew he had to keep him safe . . . for Crafter's sake.

"Weaver, come here."

The young boy pushed through the crowd and stood next to him. Gameknight handed the iron chest plate, boots, and leggings to Weaver.

"I want you to wear these," the User-that-is-not-a-user said. "Since you always seem to doing something you aren't supposed to do and getting yourself in danger to help others, perhaps it would be best if *you* wore this armor."

The boy looked up at Gameknight and smiled, then gratefully accepted the armor. He put it on quickly, then ran off to show his friends.

"Well done," Fencer said. "Weaver has been a remarkable warrior, even though he is just a boy."

"Don't judge one's courage by their size," Gameknight said. "That boy is likely braver than all of us combined." *That was a close one,* he thought to himself. *But I'm glad that I was able to help Weaver as well.*

Fencer nodded, then spoke again. "We still have three diamonds left. Should we make another sword?"

Gameknight glanced at Carver, then shook his head.

"No, I think we will be in need of a pickaxe before long," he said. "Please craft me a diamond pick. I might want to do a little digging in the middle of the upcoming battle."

"Digging?" Fencer asked.

Gameknight nodded his head.

"OK," the confused NPC replied and signaled for the diamonds to be crafted into a pickaxe. "You want to tell me why you might start digging in the middle of a battle with Herobrine and his horde?"

"Well, you see—" Gameknight began but was suddenly interrupted.

"They're back!" someone shouted from the village gates. "Some of our spies are back!"

They all dashed for the gates. Gameknight was filled with excitement; he was grateful they'd returned safely. But as he approached the gates, his spirits fell; only two black-clad villagers stood by the entrance.

"Smithy, come quick," one of the spies exclaimed.

"What is it?" Gameknight asked as he reached the villager's side.

"We saw some of Herobrine's army," he explained.

"What did you see?"

"Creepers," the spy said. "Hundreds and hundreds of them. It was as if they'd drained the land of the monsters and brought them all here."

"They have them hidden at the base of one of the Dragon's Teeth," the other explained. "A sparkly creeper is in its own cave at the base of the mountain with water running down the side."

"There are so many creepers," the first spy said, fear filling his voice. "I don't know how we can stand against them."

"And what of the rest of the army?" Gameknight asked.

"There were a few zombies in gold armor walking around on guard duty," the first spy said.

"Now they're one guard short," the other said with a smile. He reached into his inventory and pulled out a set of golden armor and tossed it to the ground. "We couldn't tell how many were hiding in the caves underground, but they must have made a huge cavern. We could hear the moans and growls of the zombies and the clattering skeletons and clicking spiders. Somehow, the monsters must have carved out a huge space down there to house them all."

"But how would monsters use tools to do that?" Fencer asked.

"I know how they did it," Gameknight said, then began to pace back and forth, thinking.

*Creepers, by the hundreds,* the User-that-is-not-a-user thought. *What would Herobrine do with them?*

"Likely, Herobrine used the creepers to carve out the caverns," Gameknight explained. "I think he's doing that all across the Overworld as he gathers monsters for this battle."

"He'll have a lot more monsters than before—I'm sure of it," the spy said. "We'll be outnumbered five-to-one if not worse. What are we going to do?"

The weight of responsibility felt overwhelming. Gameknight found it hard to breathe. All of the NPCs were looking at him as if he could pull some magical solution out of the air and solve this problem, but with the number of monsters Herobrine had, especially all those creepers . . . it seemed hopeless.

"If only we could rain fire down upon those creepers," Weaver said. "Maybe they'd just blow up and take care of themselves for us."

Suddenly, the puzzle pieces began to tumble around in his head again. Something the young NPC had said started Gameknight to think.

"Weaver, how much TNT do we have left over from the last battle with the zombie king?" Gameknight asked.

"We have a lot," the boy replied. "I know you told us to use it all on those zombies in the desert, but I had everyone hold back in case it proved useful later."

Gameknight smiled a huge smile as the pieces of the puzzle began to fall into place. But his whole plan hinged on one critical thing . . . the creepers.

"What are you smiling about?" Fencer asked. "You look a little crazy."

"You figured it out, didn't you, child?" the Oracle asked.

Gameknight nodded his blocky head.

"You know how to beat them?" Farmer asked.

"Yep, but it's gonna be extremely dangerous," Gameknight replied. "We'll be walking on a razor's edge, and any misstep will plunge us into disaster. Everyone must do as I say, or Herobrine and his massive horde of monsters will roll over us like an avalanche." He began speaking louder so everyone could hear him. "This is going to be incredibly dangerous. If any villager wants to leave now, I understand, but Smithy of the Two-Swords is staying to see this through."

Gameknight looked at the anxious faces of the villagers. As one, they all took a step closer.

"We aren't going anywhere," Carver said, his axe in his hands.

"I thought as much," Gameknight said. "Here's what we're going to do . . ."

Gameknight explained the plan, sketching diagrams on the ground with the point of his new diamond sword. As he described the strategy, the villagers nodded their heads and whispered to each other, adding an idea here and there. But when he was done with the explanation, Carver spoke up.

"Your plan hinges on the fact that the massive army of creepers is not involved in the battle. How is that going to be true?"

Some of the villagers scowled at Carver for insulting the great Smithy of the Two-Swords, but rather than looking away, Carver kept his gaze on Gameknight. The User-that-is-not-a-user smiled at the stocky NPC and moved next to him. He patted him on the back.

"Carver is right," Gameknight said. "I appreciate his willingness to ask the hard question. That is an important trait in a leader."

"A *leader*?" one of the elders scoffed.

"That's right, a leader," Gameknight replied. "I want Carver leading the defense of Midnight Bridge. He will make sure the monsters do not cross the Great Chasm, and I'm confident he will be successful."

Carver looked shocked, but pressed the point again.

"I'm happy to lead that group, but you didn't answer the question. How are you going to keep the creepers from joining the battle?"

"While all of you are preparing for battle, I'm going out there to have a little chat with the creeper king."

He smiled at Fencer, then pointed to pile of gold zombie armor. Gameknight picked it up and put it into his inventory. "I'm going to sneak in there and convince Oxus that it's in his best interests to take his creepers and just go away."

"Just go away?" Carver asked, astonished.

"That's right," Gameknight replied. "When I'm done, I'll meet you at the bridge, so you better be ready."

He then turned and walked through the village gates and into the sandy desert.

"Smithy be crazy, that's for sure," one of the villagers said, the rest of them nodding their square heads, many of them repeating the phrase as they started preparations for the battle that was quickly approaching.

# CHAPTER 26
# MEETING OF KINGS

**H**erobrine stood at the mouth of the tunnel that yawned open between the peaks of Dragon's Teeth. He glared down into the darkness, his eyes giving off a harsh, white glare like twin searchlights. Below, huge numbers of monsters milled about, each trying to find room in the cramped chamber so that their feet were not stepped on by another monster's claws. All of the creatures were incredibly uncomfortable, but that was no concern to Herobrine. The job of these monsters was to obey him, even if it meant their own destruction.

Now, only a small number of creatures were still trickling into Dragon's Teeth from the surrounding area. Herobrine had successfully drained the area of monsters, and now the rest of his forces were clustered together in zombie-towns all across the Overworld. Soon, they would arrive, but the monsters would not march to this cavern. No, the Endermen would teleport with them in their arms, bringing the rest of Herobrine's army to Dragon's

Teeth where they would gather before the final assault on the villagers.

Without the countless creepers he'd exploded, Herobrine could have never built all of these zombie-towns, and likely the villagers would have figured out what he was doing. Finally, the usefulness of the creepers had been found.

He stepped into the tunnel and followed the steps that led to the bottom of the passage. It was a steep tunnel, littered with the remains of many zombies and skeletons at the bottom that had not taken care of their footing while they followed the path. Herobrine had no fear of falling, however. If he were to stumble, he could just easily teleport away to a safe location.

The bottom of the sloping tunnel finally turned until it extended horizontally through the stone. After a dozen blocks, it opened into a massive chamber, its far side now lost in the haze of Minecraft. Streams of lava fell from the ceiling as well as from the walls, lighting the cavern in a warm orange glow. Smoke and ash drifted through the air, creating a gray mist that smelled acrid and luscious.

The floor of the cavern was pockmarked with craters, leaving very few places where the ground was actually flat and smooth. This was how all the zombie-towns appeared, as the explosive fists of the creepers did an unpredictable job at carving the chamber floor, even though they still opened up a lot of space in a short amount of time.

Moving to the right side of the zombie-town, he entered a small chamber that had been carved into the wall just for him. Waiting within the alcove were the monster kings and queen: Oxus, Shaikulud, and Erebus. A small pool of lava glowed in the corner, casting long shadows of the trio on the rough-hewn walls. The sparks that danced across the creeper king's body covered the walls with a flickering light. It created an almost magical atmosphere. That, mixed with the deep purple from Shaikulud's eight spidery eyes, caused the chamber to be filled with color and light.

Herobrine stood before his three leaders and smiled. He had created all of these with his artificially intelligent viral powers, altering the lines of Minecraft code to suit his own needs. They were each unique and magnificent. Erebus, the king of the Endermen, had been given a thirst for destruction and the desire to make all NPCs suffer. Shaikulud has been created to control all the other spiders and force them to do Herobrine's will. Her obedience to his commands was a powerful tool. And lastly, Oxus, the king of the creepers, was given part of Herobrine's intelligence, so that he could make the rest of the creepers a little smarter and more vicious. Each had a different aspect of the virus's personality, and together, the three of them were surely invincible.

"It is time for me to divulge my battle plans, as each of you have a critical part to play," Herobrine explained.

"How is it that this gigantic cavern happens to be under the four mountains you call Dragon's Teeth?" Oxus asked, his body glowing bright as he spoke.

"There are caverns all across Minecraft," Herobrine explained. "A creeper that spends most of his time underground should know this."

"But these caverns have a sulfurous smell to them," Oxus continued.

"It's from the lava," Herobrine replied.

"The lava?" Oxus asked suspiciously. The creeper king glanced at Erebus and Shaikulud, then back to Herobrine. "And where are the rest of the creepers I left with you?"

"Sadly, they perished in a battle with that blacksmith," Herobrine lied.

He didn't want the creeper king to know how many of his subjects he'd used to create all the zombie-towns.

"The vile NPC figured out a way to cause the creepers to detonate. He ignited them by the hundreds, and then just stood there and watched them explode. We collected their gunpowder, but it was a tragic atrocity that will be avenged."

Oxus moved to the corner of the chamber and found a large pile of gunpowder. He allowed all of the gray powder to fall into his inventory. Herobrine smiled as the creeper king returned; the foolish king didn't realize that was the gunpowder that had been left behind after the creepers had carved this massive zombie-town out of the flesh of Minecraft. Even with Herobrine's added intelligence, creepers were still pretty dumb.

"Our battle with the blacksmith and his NPCs draws near," Herobrine explained. "Each of you will have a critical part to play in this battle."

Herobrine moved to stand in front of the king of the Endermen.

"Erebus, you will command the main force against the NPCs. You will have all the zombies and skeletons and most of the spiders." He moved to Shaikulud. "Spider queen, you will take your best fighters around the edge of the battle. You are to find that old hag and destroy her. I fear that her presence threatens what we wish to accomplish for the monsters of Minecraft. She must be destroyed!"

His eyes glowed bright with anger as he thought about the ancient woman.

"And what of the creepers?" Oxus asked.

Herobrine's anger slowly receded, his eyes dimming.

"Ah, yes, the creepers," the Maker said. "Your part is the most important. While we distract them by battling with the villagers from the north, you are to lead your creepers south, across that obsidian bridge, and sneak up behind the villagers. You will have your creepers charge forward until your monsters are standing shoulder to shoulder with the villagers, then they are to all detonate at once." Herobrine's eyes began glowing again. "With your hundreds of creepers, none of the villagers will survive. It guarantees our success."

"But . . . not for my creepers," Oxus objected.

"Did I not create you from nothing?" Herobrine roared.

"Yes, Maker."

"And did you not pledge yourself to me, to do as I commanded?" Herobrine added.

"Yes, Maker," Oxus hissed, his body keeping its bright glow.

"Then you will do as I command," Herobrine said. "I could always replace you with another creeper king. Is that necessary?"

"No, Maker," Oxus replied meekly, his head lowered. "I will do as you command."

"I knew you would," Herobrine replied with a wry smile.

Closing his eyes for a moment, Herobrine teleported to the entrance of the small room.

"I will send an Enderman to you when it is time for your monsters to move out," he said as he glared at the three leaders. "Do you all understand your responsibilities?"

The monster kings and queen nodded their heads.

"Good, see that your troops are ready. Victory is at hand!" Herobrine laughed a malicious laugh as he disappeared, then materialized atop one of the Dragon's Teeth. "Soon, blacksmith, all of your pitiful villagers will be destroyed, and there will be nothing to stop me from spreading across the Overworld, destroying everything as I go until there is nothing left." He laughed again, this time his cackles making the very fabric of Minecraft cringe.

# CHAPTER 27
# OXUS

Gameknight stepped carefully out of the birch forest and across the stone clearing that led to Dragon's Teeth. He had to hide in a tree for an hour as a squad of zombies moved through the forest on a routine patrol. But rather than do a good job at searching for intruders, the monsters just found a shady spot to rest and complain about the cramped conditions in the zombie-town. Eventually, the monsters left, allowing Gameknight to descend from the leafy canopy and proceed toward his destination.

He could easily spot the mountain with the lava running down the side. The fiery light from the molten stone shaded everything in a warm orange glow, even in the sunlight. Opposite this peak, Gameknight saw another rocky spire whose side was covered with water. That must be the one.

Stepping out of the forest, he moved carefully into the open, the golden zombie armor he now wore, complete with shining gold helmet, reflecting the afternoon sun, throwing spots of light down around him on the stone ground. He had the urge to sprint from cover to cover, but the User-that-is-not-a-user knew that would instantly give him away. Instead, he tried to copy the motion of the other zombies.

Holding his arms out in front of him, he shuffled forward, stiff-legged, and moved clumsily across the open terrain, toward the water-drenched mountain. At one point, a group of zombies looked at him. He turned his chest just the smallest amount to reflect the sun off his metallic chest plate and into the faces of the decaying monsters. They turned away, rather than continue to stare into the bright reflection, their curiosity defeated by the inconvenient glare of the sun.

When he reached the back of the mountain, Gameknight lowered his arms and crouched. He was certain that none of the monsters could see him. With the gold sword still in his hand, the User-that-is-not-a-user sprinted around the perimeter of the Tooth, looking for the cave. As he rounded the back, an orange light could be seen spilling out onto the rocky ground. Instantly, he knew it was lava and that he had to move carefully; it would be a bad time to try swimming in the molten stone.

Approaching the glowing spot, Gameknight saw the light was coming from a cave that had been carved into the side of the mountain. In a crouch, the User-that-is-not-a-user approached slowly, trying to step as quietly as possible. In the clunky gold armor, it was difficult; the metallic plating clanked against each other, no matter how carefully he moved.

Cautiously, he crept to the edge of the cave and peered inside. It seemed empty. A stream of lava fell from the ceiling, forming a small pool in the far corner of the chamber. The walls and floor were uneven, as if formed by detonated TNT, and there were pockets and alcoves masked in shadows.

Putting aside his golden sword, Gameknight drew his iron and diamond blades, then stepped into the cave. There was no creeper king anywhere in sight. He moved to the back of the chamber and checked the shadowy corners. As he searched, Gameknight noticed the walls had become illuminated with flickering blue and red light.

"Creepers have an incredible sense of smell," a hissing voice said from behind.

Gameknight turned and found the creeper king, Oxus, standing in the entrance to the cave.

"I was able to smell you before you entered this cave," the sparkling creeper said. "Well, not really smell, but I noticed the *absence* of stink around you. These decaying zombies have such a terribly foul odor about them, but you lack that stench. So, I knew you weren't a zombie, even though you wore that useless armor."

The creeper took a step closer and began to glow, as if getting ready to explode.

"I did not come here to fight with you, Oxus," Gameknight said.

"So, you know my name," the creeper king replied. "By the look of your two swords, I can only assume I have the honor of facing Smithy, the blacksmith I've heard so much about."

Gameknight nodded.

"So you say you are not here to kill me," Oxus said.

"No, I've come to talk with you," Gameknight replied. "You know a huge battle looms on the horizon and will be upon us soon."

"Of course," the creeper hissed. "So what?"

"I don't think you want to participate in this foolishness, Oxus," Gameknight said. "You know Herobrine treats your creepers as if they were disposable."

"As do your villagers," the creeper king snapped.

"Only when we are threatened," Gameknight replied. "Herobrine has already destroyed hundreds and hundreds of your creepers." He tapped the tip of his iron sword on the cavern wall. "How do you think he made this cave? Look at the shape. He ignited one of your creepers to carve this out of the mountain."

"What of it?" the creeper asked, his glowing body slowly dimming.

"He did the same with the zombie-town that I'm sure is under Dragon's Teeth. But he did not stop there. Herobrine created many zombie-towns all across the Overworld, and he forced your creepers to detonate to make these caverns. He did it without any consideration of the lives he was extinguishing." Gameknight took a step closer, lowering his swords. "Your Maker is destroying your subjects just to satisfy his violent appetite, and you know it! He will likely sacrifice your creepers to destroy the villagers, and yet you still follow him. That makes you as bad as Herobrine."

The creeper glared at Gameknight999, the accusation making the monster glow bright with rage. Gradually, Oxus calmed down and allowed his ignition process to slowly reverse.

"I could easily call for the zombies to capture you," the creeper king said. "If I were to give you over to Herobrine, I would be a hero."

"But do you think that would stop the war?" Gameknight asked. "You know just as well as I do that Herobrine would continue with his plan, which would lead to the pointless destruction of your creepers." Now he had to gamble. "I bet his plan is to send your creepers across the bridge, to sneak up behind the NPCs army . . . am I right?"

The creeper king looked at Gameknight in shock and amazement.

"I thought so," the User-that-is-not-a-user added. "He will destroy all your followers just to satisfy his lust for violence. Is that what you want? Are you really like him? Do you care so little for your own kind?"

"Hmm . . ." Oxus mused. He gazed at the ground and considered Gameknight's words.

"I know you question the logic behind this war," Gameknight stated.

"Really . . . and what else do you think you know?" Oxus asked.

"That you have found a series of tunnels under a massive volcano," Gameknight guessed; he hoped he was right. "The lava that flows down the side of this mountain spills into the ocean. You are planning on building your creeper hive under this mountain. In a huge cavern deep underground, you store the gunpowder from the older creepers that give the last bit of their lives to enlarge the hive."

"How could you know this, blacksmith?" the creeper king snapped.

Gameknight smiled.

"I know much," he said as he put away his swords.

Oxus looked surprised as Gameknight put away his weapons, then took off the stinking gold armor and tossed it to the ground, while still keeping the golden helmet on his head.

"You are not like Herobrine," the User-that-is-not-a-user said. "Violence and suffering is not what you crave. Peace and solitude is all that you want; a place where the young creepers can gnaw at the coal ore in the walls until their white spots fill in with black; a place where you can honor your ancestors and live a quiet life without violence and suffering." He took a step closer to the creeper. "Yes, Oxus, king of the creepers, I know much about you."

"How can you know these things?" the monster replied in shock.

"If I were to explain, you would not understand," Gameknight said. "But you must believe me when I say you must leave this place with your creepers, and go hide under that hill in your creeper hive."

"Why should I trust you?" Oxus asked. "Maybe you are trying to lure my creepers into a trap."

"I will show you why you should trust me." Gameknight reached up and removed his helmet, then tossed it aside.

"You . . . you're not a villager . . . you're something else," Oxus said in shock.

"I'm a user, the first user in Minecraft, and I share this secret with you so that you'll believe my words," Gameknight said. "None of the villagers know that I'm not the blacksmith, Smithy. He was killed in the battle with the zombie king. I've been posing as him to keep them together and keep them fighting against Herobrine and his war of insanity. If they knew I was a fraud, the NPC army would fall apart and Herobrine would win. That evil virus could sweep across Minecraft, destroying everything, and the villagers could do nothing to stop him."

Oxus began to pace back and forth across the entrance to the cave, his body glowing bright, then becoming dim again as he contemplated this revelation.

"You now have the power to destroy thousands of lives and be just like Herobrine," Gameknight said. "Or you can be a creature that values life. It's your choice to make."

Oxus took a step toward Gameknight999, but the User-that-is-not-a-user held his ground and did not retreat. The creeper came closer and closer until he brushed past him and moved to the back of the chamber.

"You have given me much to consider," Oxus said. "I have decided that I will not call the guards. You are free to go while I consider your words."

"Will you take your creepers away from this battle?" Gameknight asked.

"I have not decided," the creeper king replied. "You will know when the battle starts."

"Fair enough," he replied.

"It is time for you to leave," the creeper said.

"There is one more thing," Gameknight said. "In the future, we will meet again. I won't know we have met before and will be confused, but you should believe me when I tell you that I have never see you before."

The creeper king looked confused, but allowed him to continue.

"You must give me a message," Gameknight said, remembering what Oxus had said to him in the treasure room of the creeper hive. "You must tell me these words, exactly as I say them."

"Fine, I'll play your game, user." Oxus said. "Tell me."

"You must say, 'Have faith in yourself, and don't worry what other people think. You must do what is right for those you care about, even if it means stepping aside for another to lead. Friends and family are more important, and sometimes the sword is not the answer.' Now repeat it to me."

The monster repeated the words multiple times until Gameknight was satisfied.

"We need not be enemies, Oxus. We can choose the path we wish to follow," Gameknight said. "Sometimes, the sword is not the answer."

"Perhaps," the monster replied.

Bending down, Gameknight retrieved the golden armor and put it on again. The zombie stench on it almost made him gag, but he forced himself to don the stinking disguise.

"When we see each other again," Gameknight repeated, "we need not be enemies."

The creeper did not answer; he just stared at him, waiting for him to leave. Gameknight nodded farewell, then turned and moved to the cave opening.

"Wait, if you are not Smithy of the Two-Swords, then what is your name?" the king of the creepers asked.

"I'm Gameknight999, the User-that-is-not-a-user," he replied, then turned and headed for the Midnight Bridge.

## CHAPTER 28

# ROLLING THE DICE

Gameknight moved quickly and quietly through the birch forest. He could see the sun getting lower and lower in the sky, and he really didn't want to be out here in the darkness with all these monsters nearby. After all, nighttime was monster time in Minecraft.

He wove around the white-barked trees, sprinting as fast as he could with the cumbersome armor restricting his motion. The gold zombie disguise creaked and clanked as he moved, making enough noise to wake the dead, but fortunately for him, the moans of the zombies and clattering of the skeletons was easily drowning out the sound.

Glancing over his shoulder, he could no longer see Dragon's Teeth, as the trees and hills were now blocking his view. It allowed him to relax just a bit.

"I'm probably far enough away to get rid of this," he muttered to himself.

Gratefully, he took off the putrid armor and cast it into a bush, then put on his dark brown leather armor . . . well, it wasn't really his, it was Smithy's.

It was big armor to wear, and earlier, he hadn't really been sure if he could fill it . . . or even if he should. Gameknight hated living this lie, posing as Smithy and deceiving the people that had now become his friends. But at that moment, in that desert battle in the narrow mountain pass, the User-that-is-not-a-user hadn't had time to think; all he'd had time to do was react and help those that needed it. And at that moment, in the heat of battle, the villagers had needed Smithy more than they needed Gameknight999. They still did.

He sighed as he kicked the golden helmet further into the shrub and placed the iron helmet on his head. With his disguise again complete, he moved through the forest quickly, heading back toward the Midnight Bridge. Glancing to the west, Gameknight noticed the horizon beginning to blush with a crimson hue as the sun began to settle itself behind the horizon. Shifting to a sprint again, he dashed through the forest, shooting past birch trees and leaping over leafy shrubs. He wanted to get back to the bridge before it was dark; he'd rather not be accidently shot by his own archers.

By the time the sun had completely settled below the horizon, and the sparkling blanket of stars had spread itself across the sky, Gameknight could see the dark bridge in the distance. Torches had been placed all along the edges, casting enough light to see anyone attempting to cross. It lit up the bridge span, making it glow with a subtle purple hue. Gameknight knew that was from the sparkling lavender particles that were embedded in the obsidian.

He ran quickly to the end and stopped to view the defenders' progress. On the far side, he saw the stocky form of Carver and at least fifty of their finest warriors. They'd been assigned the unfortunate task of holding this bridge from all monster attacks and refusing to allow any of Herobrine's forces from crossing it. Likely, this would soon be the location of a terrifying, pitched battle, but for now, all was quiet. Slowing to a walk, Gameknight crossed the obsidian structure.

"Someone's coming," a lookout called.

Instantly, the villagers took their places, climbing atop archer towers and along fortified walls that lined their side of the Great Chasm.

"It's Smithy of the Two-Swords," the lookout shouted.

As Gameknight approached, he saw the defenders visibly relax as they lowered their bows and put away their blades. When he reached the far side, someone broke a series of cobblestone blocks, allowing him to pass through the defensive wall and reach the other side of the Chasm.

Carver and Weaver approached, both of them looking relieved and a little surprised at his return.

"You survived?" Weaver said with a smile on his square face.

"Did you talk with your creeper friend?" Carver asked.

The User-that-is-not-a-user nodded his head. "Yep, I spoke with the king of the creepers at length," Gameknight replied.

"Are they going to join the battle?" Carver asked, a hint of fear in his voice.

"I'm not sure," he replied. "I tried to make a convincing case why the creepers should just stay out of this battle, but I'm not sure if Oxus believed me. One thing I know for sure: if they're going to join the fight, I think we'll know about it right away."

"Why is that?" one of the warriors asked.

"Because their plan is to come across this bridge with a couple hundred creepers so they can sneak up behind our forces," Gameknight replied, "and destroy everyone."

"Did you say a *couple hundred* creepers?" someone asked.

"Yep," he replied.

"Why don't we just make the creepers detonate on the bridge, destroying it?" someone suggested.

"Because their explosions won't even make a scratch in the obsidian," he replied. "But they will certainly harm our defenses . . . and us."

An uncomfortable silence filled the air. Gameknight was sure the villagers were weighing their options and deciding if they should stay and fight or run. To help them decide, the User-that-is-not-a-user climbed to the top of the fortified wall, drew his two swords, and held them over his head for all to see.

"Rest assured, I am going nowhere," he said in a confident voice. "None of Herobrine's mob is getting past any of us. We have the defenses and the better position *and* the better plan. No stinking zombies are going to take our bridge from us!"

The warriors cheered, and worried scowls were quickly replaced by confident looks of courage. Weaver climbed to the top of the wall and stood at Gameknight's side.

"You think you really convinced the creeper king to leave?" Weaver asked, the torchlight reflecting off his new iron armor, making him glow.

"I can't be sure," Gameknight replied. "Oxus, the creeper king, is hard to read. I sensed some anger in him, but wasn't sure if it was directed at Herobrine, or me."

"You *do* have a way of making monsters hate you," Carver said.

The NPCs all chuckled.

"Weaver, you have all the leftover TNT? " Gameknight asked.

"Yep," the boy replied. "Just like you said."

"I don't get it," Carver said. "Why don't we just break this bridge so the creepers can't get across?"

"Because Weaver and I have a little job on the other side of the Chasm," Gameknight replied. "And I'd rather not get stuck over there with Herobrine's army."

"What do you *think* the creepers will do?" Carver asked.

"I don't know. We just have to roll the dice and see what we get," Gameknight replied.

"'Roll the dice'?" Carver asked.

"'See what we get'?" Weaver added. "Sometimes, you're so strange."

Gameknight laughed, then moved to help some of the warriors to reinforce the defenses.

# CHAPTER 29
# OXUS MAKES HIS CHOICE

Suddenly, an NPC came running out of the birch forest and across the obsidian bridge.

"They're coming! They're coming!" the villager exclaimed.

By the color of his smock, which was charcoal gray with a yellow stripe, Gameknight could tell he was a cobbler. Though he was a few years older, the NPC reminded him of the cobbler Gameknight had met the last time he'd been with Crafter and his friends.

Thinking about all of them brought back a chilling fear: If he messed this up, some of his best friends might never be born. Casting a glance at Weaver, Gameknight shuddered.

*I have to keep him safe*, Gameknight thought. *Not just him—every*one.

The cobbler reached their defenses, sprinted through an opening in the wall, then headed straight toward Gameknight999.

"Slow down, Cobbler," Gameknight said. "Take a breath."

The NPC smiled up at him, paused to take two or three deep breaths, then spoke.

"They're coming, Smithy. The monsters are coming," Cobbler said.

"Creepers . . . is it creepers?" Carver asked.

"I'm not sure," Cobbler replied. "I heard the zombies from the tree I was hiding in, then I saw a lot of creatures moving between the branches. There was a lot of green, but I didn't stick around to see what kind of monsters were coming. I just wanted to get out of there."

"You did well, Cobbler," Gameknight said. "Go sit down and rest. I suspect we'll need your sword for the monster storm that is heading our way."

He nodded, then moved to a sand dune and sat.

"Are the defenses ready?" Gameknight asked as he glanced around at the end of the bridge.

"The wall and archer towers are complete," Carver said. "But I fear the archers will have difficulty firing on the monsters. There are a lot of supports made of obsidian along the sides of the bridge. Getting a clear shot will be difficult."

"I think I have a solution," Gameknight replied.

Jumping off the wall, he pulled out the diamond pickaxe from his inventory and moved to the middle of the bridge. With all his strength, he began to chisel away at the supports, opening the sides of the bridge so the archers would have clear access. He moved closer to their defensive wall and removed more of the supports, creating large openings in the side of the bridge. When he was satisfied, he returned to their side of the Chasm, then moved to Carver's side.

"There's one more thing you need to do," the User-that-is-not-a-user said to the stocky NPC.

He held out the pickaxe, extending it to Carver.

"No matter what happens, the monsters can't cross this bridge. If you need to break it to ensure that, then do it. This diamond pick will make it easy."

"Maybe you should give it to one of the diggers, or maybe a real warrior," the stocky NPC said. "I'm just a carver with nothing to carve. I'm the wrong person to trust with this responsibility."

"No, you are the right person to trust. I can feel it," Gameknight said. "I have no doubt you will find what you should be carving with your axe, eventually, but for now, I need your sword and maybe this pickaxe."

He took a step closer to him and spoke in a low voice.

"I learned recently that if you want people to have faith in you, then first you must have faith in yourself. If I can believe in myself and lead the army against this overwhelming foe, then you can hold this end of the bridge." He looked up into his deep, green eyes. "I believe in you . . . can you do the same?"

Before Carver could answer, one of the NPCs yelled, "They're here!"

Gameknight turned slowly, dreading what he'd see. If it were Oxus and all his creepers, then likely, their army would be defeated, if not now, then in the desert facing Herobrine and his massive army.

Gameknight realized he'd closed his eyes. The sorrowful moans of the zombies drifted across the Great Chasm and filled his ears with their intolerable sadness. Hesitantly, he opened them. On the other side of the bridge, emerging from the darkness of the forest, he saw a host of zombies, skeletons, and spiders, but no creepers. Oxus had done it . . . he'd taken his creepers and left the field of battle.

"No creepers!" Carver shouted as he clapped the User-that-is-not-a-user on the back.

The NPCs cheered.

"Get to your positions," Gameknight said. "We have to hold this bridge at all costs!"

"SMITHY!" the NPCs shouted and took their positions amid their fortifications.

Gameknight jumped off the wall and landed cat-like on the dark bridge. He stepped out in front of their defenses and glared at the monster horde. There were likely a hundred of them, outnumbering the defenders two-to-one. It didn't matter how many monsters were over there; they could not pass. Gameknight had business to attend to out there on the battlefield, for he had his own little surprise for Herobrine and his monsters, and he needed this bridge to get there.

When they saw his two swords, the monsters roared, both in anger and excitement. Spiders clicked their mandibles together as the zombies growled hungrily. Endermen cackled with evil delight and skeleton bones clattered together. The noise was nearly deafening.

Gripping the hilts firmly, he banged his swords together. They made a metallic clanking sound, ironically enough, like an iron hammer hitting against an anvil. He glared at the monsters that congregated at the far end of the bridge.

"You want some?" Gameknight shouted, "Then come and get it."

The warriors behind him cheered and banged their swords on the sides of the bridge, creating a rhythmical pounding sound that vibrated along the length of the bridge. And then the moon rose above the horizon and cast a silvery light on the scene. It made both sides eerily quiet as they gazed at each other.

"COME ON, MONSTERS," he screamed, his thundering voice startling both sides. "LET'S DANCE!"

"Smithy be crazy!" someone shouted from behind.

"No," Weaver said. "Smithy isn't crazy . . . Smithy be *mad*!"

And as if on cue, the monsters charged, but Gameknight999 stood his ground and waited.

# CHAPTER 30
# BATTLE AT MIDNIGHT BRIDGE

The monsters charged across the bridge, snarling and growling. But Gameknight stood his ground, motionless . . . waiting. It clearly unnerved some of the monsters at the front, for their hateful eyes began to fill with uncertainty as they wondered why an NPC wouldn't turn in fear at the sight of them approaching.

Suddenly, Carver leapt off the fortified wall and landed with a great thud that made the bridge shake ever-so-slightly. He moved next to Gameknight999 and stood, motionless and ready.

"Not sure if this is such a good idea for you," Gameknight said.

"If it's OK for you, then it's OK for me," Carver snapped as he drew his iron sword and waited for the mob. "I believe I can make a difference right here, next to you."

"OK then."

The growling horde charged across the bridge. When they reached the middle, Gameknight held his two swords over his head.

"NOW!" the User-that-is-not-a-user yelled.

Suddenly, groups of hidden archers climbed to the top of sand dunes on the left and right sides of the bridge. They fired into the openings that Gameknight had carved in the side of the bridge with the diamond pickaxe. Arrows streaked through the darkness, each making a *whizzing* sound, then a *thunk* when they found a monster body.

Zombies and skeletons screamed out in pain as they flashed red with damage. Arrows flew back at the archers, but the sand dunes and archers were cloaked in darkness, far from any of the torches lighting the bridge. The skeletons could not tell where to shoot, so they just fired haphazardly into the desert night, hoping to hit something.

The horde was getting closer.

"Get ready!" Gameknight shouted as he gripped his swords firmly.

The monsters moved past the midpoint and charged at Gameknight and Carver, their howls of rage echoing off the walls of the Great Chasm. They moved forward even faster, reaching the next set of gaps in the side of the bridge.

"Fire!"

The archers took aim on the next openings, firing as fast as they could at the monstrous flood. Spiders screeched in pain and zombies howled out in rage. But the monsters still did not slow; they continued to advance across Midnight Bridge.

And then finally, they reached Gameknight999 and Carver. Instantly, the User-that-is-not-a-user went into battle mode. He stopped thinking and only reacted. Moving to the left, he slashed at a zombie that was charging toward Carver. The monster flashed red, then turned toward Gameknight, but he was already gone. He shifted to the right and slashed at a pair of spiders, driving his blades down with every ounce of strength he had in him.

Monsters fell all around them, Gameknight destroying three for every one Carver took down.

"Ahh!" the NPC yelled.

A spider had sliced into Carver's leather leggings, and had sunk its claw into his leg. The villager flashed red as he took damage, then brought his sword down clumsily upon the spider. Gameknight rushed to his side, but was blocked by a pair of zombies. He slashed at the decaying creatures as he watched the spider reach up and jab at Carver's hand with its dark, curved claw. The razor-sharp tip caused the NPC to drop his sword. The villager stepped back as the spider advanced.

"Carver . . . run!" Gameknight shouted.

But the NPC just shook his head, refusing to retreat. Reaching into his inventory, he pulled out his axe. The razor-sharp tool gleamed in the torchlight, the polished surface reflecting the surroundings like the finest mirror.

Carver gripped the handle with both hands and started to carve. He chopped at the spider, hitting it twice before the monster even knew what was happening. His hands were lightning-quick, moving the axe as if it were weightless. With one great strike, Carver destroyed the spider, then went to work on one of the zombies in front of Gameknight. The decaying monster fell under Carver's assault, allowing the two comrades to stand side-by-side.

Archers continued to fire through the openings on the bridge. Warriors on the towers built on the end of the bridge poured their arrows down upon the monsters, giving quarter to none.

"Come on, Carver, let's get back behind the wall," Gameknight said as more monsters approached.

"No," the NPC snapped. "My place is here!"

Screaming as loud as he could, Carver charged at the monsters, his axe flashing through the air like a bolt of iron lightning. Gameknight smiled, then dashed forward, watching his side. The warriors behind them cheered Carver's name, then jumped down and advanced. Now, the monsters were facing rows of swords, and all looked uncertain.

"Attack!" shouted a zombie general clad in gold.

The zombie hit some of his own troops with his golden sword, encouraging them forward. The monsters advanced. Clearly they were afraid of their general, but they were also fearful of Carver.

The big NPC didn't give them any time to consider their options. With another battle cry, Carver charged forward. His axe slashed to the right, then chopped to the left. He made multiple monsters flash red with damage as he made great sweeping strokes with his weapon. The monsters tried to fall back, but there was no place to go.

Suddenly, arrows began to fall down upon the monsters from above. Glancing up, Gameknight could see Weaver leading a group of archers along the tall, arcing supports that lined each side of the bridge. They moved until they were directly over the monsters, then fired straight down upon them. The creatures were packed together so tightly that the archers just couldn't miss. Pointed missiles rained down on the monsters while Carver's axe and Gameknight's dual swords tore through them like a razor-sharp tornado.

The monsters, realizing they could not win this battle, began to retreat.

"Don't let them get away!" Gameknight cried out.

Weaver and the other kids waved down to him, then sprinted along the tall bridge supports until they were near the end of the bridge. Pulling out buckets of water, they poured them down onto the bridge from above, creating a wall of water that slowed the monsters' progress. The archers then moved to the end of the bridge and jumped to the ground. Firing their bows through the water as fast as possible, the archers struck at the monsters as they slowly waded through the blue liquid. With arrows hitting them from one side, and swords from the other, the monsters took terrible damage.

The fighting was fierce on both sides. When the monsters realized they could not escape, they fought with renewed strength. Spiders tried to climb the supports of the bridge, but were quickly brought down by NPC archers. Skeletons took aim at Gameknight and Carver, but suddenly, more archers moved to the front and silenced the bony creatures.

The last to fall were the zombies. The decaying monsters charged forward, many of them shouting at Smithy, trying to destroy him, but there were just too many swords and arrows. The green monsters slowly succumbed until only the gold-clad general remained. Feigning injury, he suddenly charged at Gameknight999, but Carver was there with a flash of iron. The monster disappeared, his golden armor clattering to the ground.

"We did it!" Weaver yelled.

A cheer rose up over the Great Chasm as the warriors cheered.

Moving through the water, Weaver and the other kids rejoined the warriors. Gameknight patted the boy on the back, then turned and faced Carver.

"You were . . . incredible," Gameknight said.

"Well, I dropped my sword back there," Carver said sheepishly. "I guess that wasn't a very good thing to do. The axe was all I had left."

"I'm glad you dropped your sword," Gameknight said. "Your axe won the day for us and allowed us to keep this bridge."

The other NPCs shouted Carver's name, many of them slapping him on the back.

"It seems you found something worthy enough to carve with that glorious axe," Gameknight said with a smile.

"He's the carver of monsters!" one of the warriors shouted.

"Carver, the carver of monsters!" the others shouted.

"Savior of Midnight Bridge!"

The stocky NPC just smiled as they shouted praise, his hand moving along the handle of his now-famous axe.

They moved back to their side of the bridge. Carver pulled out the diamond pickaxe and created a hole in the cobblestone defenses, allowing everyone to pass through. He then moved to Gameknight's side and extended the diamond pickaxe to the blacksmith.

"I think this is yours," Carver said. "You should keep it."

"No," Gameknight replied. "I need you to hold onto that pick. You have an important job to do with it still."

Carver looked at him, confused.

"You need to pass it down through your family, giving it to every male baker."

"But I don't understand," Carver replied.

"It doesn't matter," Gameknight replied. "This is the task I'm asking you to do for me. Pass it down to your baker son, then his baker son and the next and next. One of the bakers in your family tree will have an important task to do with that pickaxe, and the lives of many will depend on it. Will you do this for me?"

Carver, though he still seemed confused, nodded his head. "As you wish."

"Excellent," Gameknight replied. "Now, I must do the next task. I fear everything will rely on its success, for I'm sure the rest of the army is completely outnumbered."

"You can't go!" Carver snapped. "Your place is with the army, not out there risking your life."

"No, I won't ask anyone else to do this thing for me," Gameknight replied.

"We can do it!" snapped Weaver. "I know more about TNT than anyone else, and me and my friends are faster than everyone. We can do it, and we won't be noticed because we are so small."

"He's right," Carver added. "Your place is with the army, as their leader. I will go with Weaver and make sure they are safe."

Gameknight looked at Carver, then flashed a glance at Weaver. He could see the confidence in all their eyes, and he knew they were right.

With a sigh, the User-that-is-not-a-user nodded his head.

"You're right about most of that," Gameknight said. "Weaver and his friends will plant the surprises. But Carver, you aren't going with them."

The stocky NPC glanced at the blacksmith, confused.

"Instead, Carver, the carver of monsters will be at my side," Gameknight said. "Your axe will be better put to use out there in the desert, rather than sneaking around behind Herobrine's back. Agreed?"

"Agreed," Carver replied.

"Remember, Weaver, when you see me give you the sign, that means we're going to start, and you need to get out of there," Gameknight explained. "And you'd better be fast."

"There's no one faster than me and my friends," the young boy replied with a smile.

"OK. It's time." Gameknight gave Weaver one last look, then nodded. "Be safe."

"No problem," Weaver replied. "We'll just be solving this monster problem with a little creativity and a lot of TNT."

The boy smiled, then all the kids ran across the bridge and into the darkness. At the same time, Gameknight999 and Carver headed back northward to where the biggest battle ever seen in Minecraft would soon be fought.

## CHAPTER 31

# THEY ARRIVE

**H**erobrine paced back and forth, the light from the lava flow casting a warm orange light on the stone ground. He peered up at the four mountains that stood around him and glared, his eyes glowing bright white with frustration.

Around him stood his shadow-crafters, each shaped or shaded like their subjects. Zombiebrine was working on the monsters' claws, making them sharper, while Skeletonbrine was trying to improve the strength of the pale monsters' bows. Every chance they had, the strange creatures stopped to work on their charges, seeking to make the monsters of the night stronger and more vicious. They had already improved on the monsters significantly, but Herobrine demanded more, and those that did not deliver, like Lavabrine, were eliminated.

"Where are they?" the evil virus growled. "Those foolish Endermen should be here by now."

"They're probably gathering all your follow-erssss," Shaikulud said.

"Well, we aren't going to wait. Go in the zombie-town and tell them to all come out. It's time to start the battle that will destroy the blacksmith and all his pathetic villagers."

Herobrine turned and glared at the spider queen. "I gave you an order . . . GO!"

The fuzzy monster bowed her head, her multiple purple eyes glowing in the darkness. She turned and scurried into the hole that led down to the underground cavern. Seconds later, the sorrowful moans and growls of the monster army grew louder as they emerged out of the shadowy passage.

Herobrine teleported to a grass-covered hill nearby and glared at the monsters, his glowing eyes shining like two hate-filled beacons.

"This way, you fools!" the Maker shouted. "Come this way!"

The monsters headed toward his voice, the zombies' claws clicking on the stone ground as they shuffled away from the boiling lava and the surging waterfall. Spiders climbed out of the hole and moved quickly to the hilltop, surrounding Herobrine and keeping the zombies and skeletons from getting too close.

"Hurry, you idiots," the evil virus demanded. "I want to attack the blacksmith at dawn."

He glanced up at the square face of the partially-filled moon. The lunar body was heading down from its zenith and would meet the horizon soon.

*Perhaps I need to make an example of someone so they'll all speed up*, Herobrine thought.

He reached into his inventory and drew his iron sword. The blade scraped against the edge of the scabbard, making a metallic hissing sound like that of a mechanical snake. The nearest zombies eyed

Herobrine nervously, and some of them stepped back. He was just about to teleport into the zombie-town when a cloud of purple mist formed on the ground between the Dragon's Teeth. An Enderman with four monsters clasped to his body appeared, his long, clammy black arms holding the monsters close. He released the creatures, then disappeared to collect another load while more of his dark brothers and sisters materialized on the rocky plain, each with monsters in their grasp.

"Excellent!" Herobrine exclaimed.

Just then, one of the Endermen appeared at his side. Herobrine turned and found himself staring up at Erebus.

"You finally arrived," Herobrine said, an annoyed look on his square face.

"Some of the monsters did not want to volunteer," the Endermen king said. "We had to destroy a few to encourage the rest to come with us."

"I hope you made them suffer," the evil virus said.

Erebus smiled, then cackled with glee.

More of the dark creatures materialized all around them, depositing their monsters and quickly disappearing to get more. Slowly, across the Overworld, one zombie-town after another was drained of monsters as they were all brought to Dragon's Teeth.

Herobrine's army grew larger and larger every minute, and the Endermen began having difficulty finding places to deposit their charges. But after another ten minutes, the Endermen had finally completed their task. Herobrine's army was finally assembled.

Their leader looked down upon his troops and smiled.

"My subjects!" Herobrine shouted, waiting for the monsters to grow quiet.

Some of the zombies far from Herobrine were still growling and moaning. The Maker glanced at Erebus and pointed with his sword at the offending group. The shadowy king teleported to the monsters and pummeled them with his fists, causing them to flash red as they took damage.

"Listen to your Maker!" Erebus screeched.

The rest of the army grew quiet, no one wanting to be the next example.

"My subjects," Herobrine continued. "You are about to witness an historic event. This is the largest monster army ever formed in Minecraft. Soon, we will meet the blacksmith, Smithy, and his villagers in battle. The cowardly creepers have slinked away in the night, but a group of monsters were already sent forth to begin the battle, and since we have heard no reports, I can only assume they have been successful."

The monsters growled and clicked and clattered and screeched. Herobrine held his arms up into the air, quieting the mob.

"When we are done squashing this NPC army, we will then sweep across the Overworld, destroying all the villages. After we have exterminated all of our enemies, then Minecraft will belong to the monsters."

They cheered and growled and moaned again.

"Everyone, forward," Herobrine shouted. "It is time to start the real invasion."

The monstrous army shuffled forward, across the extreme hills biome and into the darkness. But as they moved away from Dragon's Teeth, none of them noticed the group of young boys in the forest, watching . . . and waiting.

# CHAPTER 32

# FACING THE BEAST

Gameknight and Carver ran back to the village, leaving the rest of the bridge defenders manning their defenses in case the monsters made another attempt to cross the Great Chasm. As they sprinted, the User-that-is-not-a-user felt as if he was racing the moon. The pockmarked face that floated high overhead was slowly sinking toward the horizon and would eventually bring forth the day. Gameknight wanted to be with the army in the desert when that happened, to call Herobrine to battle at dawn.

When they reached the village, the duo found it thankfully empty. That meant everything had been prepared and the army had moved out. The scouts had all returned and reported back on the massive number of monsters that had been hiding within the huge cave under Dragon's Teeth. They also found a great place for the battle, between two large sand dunes at the northern end of the Great Chasm. Gameknight had drawn out on the ground with the tip of his sword what he had wanted for the defenses, then left it to Fencer and Farmer to make it happen. Now, he hoped the villagers had reached the battlefield with enough time to construct the defenses. Without these structures, they would surely be overrun in the first monstrous charge.

Passing the village, Gameknight and Carver found a wide path of footprints heading northeast, away from the village. It wove around the green, prickly cactuses that dotted the landscape, sometimes parting to flow around the painful plants, while other times just veering away from the large clusters. The small, dried bushes had been ignored and trampled; the remnants of the brown shrubs looked like piles of ashes crushed under many boots.

The trail quickly met up with the Great Chasm and moved parallel to the jagged gash in the Overworld. As he walked, Gameknight thought about Weaver and the other kids.

"Are you OK?" Carver asked. "You look as pale as a skeleton."

"I'm just worried about Weaver and the others," Gameknight replied. "Those kids are in terrible danger because of me, and if they are unsuccessful, then we are all in big trouble."

*And if Weaver is killed while setting the trap,* Gameknight thought, *what will happen to Crafter and all his friends in his own timeline? Without Weaver's teachings in the future, then Crafter might never become skilled with fireworks and explosives. TNT had been a decisive tool in their battle against Erebus, Malacoda, and Herobrine. It was critical that Crafter's knowledge of those blocks was still there when Gameknight finally made it back to the future.*

"It was the right decision, leaving Weaver in charge of that task," Carver said reassuringly. "He knows more about TNT than anyone else. I don't care what the elders say—being young doesn't mean you're useless and can't contribute. That little NPC and his friends are braver than a lot of warriors I know, including even myself."

"I don't know about that."

"Anyway," Carver continued. "I'm sure they'll be alright. Those kids are smart and fast. They'll be OK."

"I hope so," Gameknight said.

"Look," Crafter said, pointing to a large hill with his axe.

Ahead, they could see a cobblestone structure slowly rising out of the desert. They were running up the gradual incline of a wide, tall sand dune, but as they reached the top, they could see the entire landscape before them. Just barely visible in the darkness was a cobblestone structure being frantically erected atop a large sandy hill. Torches were placed haphazardly on the structure to give the workers enough light to build upward and still not lose their footing in the gloomy night.

"Look, there's another one over there," Carver exclaimed.

As they neared, torches from another tower were just becoming visible. The second structure, like the first, was being built atop a large sand dune. The tower on the right nearly touched the end of the Great Chasm, while the tower on the left stood tall on the steeper hill. Gameknight knew that the left tower was the weak point in their defenses, and Herobrine would recognize it as well. That was where this battle would be won or lost. If their defenses didn't hold until Weaver had completed his task, then they would all likely perish under a storm of claws and fangs.

Between the two towers was a long cobblestone wall standing four blocks tall, and still growing. Like a colony of ants swarming over a discarded apple, the workers climbed all over the structure, placing blocks of stone as fast as possible. Gameknight could see walkways being added to the structure, with holes left open above the causeway where archers could fire their arrows without being exposed to the arrows of the enemy. As the wall grew, more protected positions were added for the archers. Gameknight knew that their arrows would be critical in the first stages of the battle. But when the monsters reached the wall, it would be a simple contest of swords versus claws.

Suddenly, a voice rang out, cutting through the dark desert night.

"Smithy and Carver are coming," an NPC shouted.

A cheer rang out across the desert.

Gameknight cringed; he hoped they weren't advertising their position to Herobrine, not yet—although it was likely the virus already had Endermen out there in the darkness . . . watching. Their presence here was probably not a secret.

"How did it go?" Fencer asked. "Any creepers?"

Gameknight shook his head.

"None," he replied. "Either Herobrine changed his plans and is saving the creepers for this battle, or Oxus took them away."

"I vote for the latter," Fencer said with a smile. The villagers chuckled. "We thought you were staying out there to plant the little surprises."

"Carver thought it would be better if I was here with the rest of the army," Gameknight replied. "Instead, Weaver and the other kids are doing it."

"Carver was right. That *is* a better idea," Fencer said.

"So you held the bridge?" Farmer asked.

Gameknight smiled, then placed a hand on Carver's shoulder.

"Carver here drove the monsters back almost singlehandedly," Gameknight said.

"Well, that's not really true," Carver said, embarrassed.

"Really?" Farmer replied.

"The warriors at the bridge now call him Carver, the carver of monsters," Gameknight said proudly. "He saved a lot of lives with that axe of his."

"Is that true?" Farmer said suspiciously.

The stocky NPC ignored the comment and moved off to help with building the walls, the old village leader eyeing him as he went.

"You need to take it easy on him," Gameknight said to Farmer. "He is likely the greatest warrior you have in your village, and you should show him a little more respect."

"The greatest warrior . . . ha!" the old NPC replied. "If he was a great warrior, then he'd know how to use that sword of his. But as it is, I always must assign someone to watch his back in battle."

"You will have a different opinion of him after this battle, I can assure you."

"We'll see about that," Farmer added, then turned and moved toward the far tower to direct some of the workers.

Gameknight looked at Fencer and shrugged.

"Is everything almost ready?" Gameknight asked as he peered up at the moon. The silvery body was approaching the horizon; it would be dawn soon.

"The walls and towers will be done before sunrise," his friend reported. "Villagers are digging holes all throughout the desert. Hopefully, some of the monsters will fall in and not be able to get out."

"Good thinking," Gameknight said.

He reached up and stuffed a finger under his helmet to scratch his head, then glanced back at Fencer, a worried look on his face.

"I know what you're thinking," Fencer objected softly before Gameknight could even speak. "We need Smithy now more than ever. Look around you . . . these villagers are terrified. They all know if Weaver and the other youngsters fail, then none of them will survive this battle."

"But don't you think they deserve to know the truth?" Gameknight whispered.

"They deserve to know that which will help them the most," a scratchy voice said from behind.

The User-that-is-not-a-user turned and found the Oracle standing right behind him.

"How'd you get behind me?" Gameknight asked.

"I can move pretty quietly when I want to," the old woman replied with a smile.

"So you agree with Fencer?" Gameknight asked.

"You seek to unburden your soul, to free yourself of guilt?" the Oracle said.

Gameknight nodded.

"All of us are here for a reason," she said. "Myself, I'm here to restore balance with my light-crafters. Carver over there," she pointed to the stocky NPC with her crooked, wooden cane. "He is here to find himself and learn that he is a leader. Your friend Fencer is here to right the wrongs he perpetrated on you after first coming to his village."

The NPC looked to the ground, ashamed.

"He rights these wrongs through the best way possible . . . through friendship with you." The Oracle gave Fencer a smile that seemed to lighten his burdened soul. "Everyone here, at this moment in time, is here for a reason. That is the way Minecraft works; it draws people together so that they can appreciate their strengths and face their weaknesses, so that they can find the limits of their abilities and figure out how they can go a little further."

She lowered her voice to the faintest whisper. "And for you, Gameknight999, this is especially true. You are here to protect your friends who exist in two different times: those that surround you here and those that exist a long time from now. I'm sure you know the lives of your friends in the future are dependent on what happens here, in this time. If we fail, then they may never exist, and you feel responsible for them."

Gameknight nodded his boxy head.

"So Minecraft has brought you here, at this exact moment, for one reason," the Oracle said as she took a step closer to him.

"What's that?" Gameknight asked, an almost desperate tone to his voice.

"You are here because you can endure these hardships in silence," the Oracle said. "You can do what is necessary without the need for fame or recognition. You can face these monsters, and perhaps even face Herobrine himself, with no thought for yourself, only for your friends. Your unwavering dedication to those around you is the wall that

Herobrine cannot break, and that will tip the balance in this war. That is why you're here."

Gameknight reached up and wiped a tear from his eye as he stared at the old woman.

"You think I can do it?" he asked. "You think I can lead these people through this battle and keep them safe?"

"Not all of them," the old woman replied. "War is dangerous business, and people get hurt . . . or worse. None of us can change that. But what I do believe is that you can lead these people and keep them trying when it appears all is lost. And in that darkest of moments, when it seems there is no hope, that is when your strength will shine through, and Herobrine will be the one to feel the fear of defeat."

"You really think so?" Gameknight asked.

The old woman nodded her head, making her long, gray hair fall across her wrinkled face. She pulled the strands aside and smiled at him.

Suddenly, a voice called out from one of the towers.

"They're here!"

"I guess it's time we found out," Fencer said, then slapped Gameknight on the back with a laugh.

He nodded, then glanced over at the light-crafters frantically working, their hands plunged into the ground.

*I hope this works*, Gameknight thought.

*Have faith, child*, a voice said in his head as beautiful melodic tones filled his mind. He turned and found the Oracle smiling at him, her gray eyes bright with hope.

Running up the sandstone stairs, he took his place at the center of the fortified wall. And as the sun slowly rose in the east, splashing bands of crimson and orange across the sky, Gameknight saw the massive body of monsters approaching. They were so close together, it was as if they were one giant beast, and he was staring right into its face.

Gameknight sighed, then drew his diamond sword with his right hand and his iron sword with his left.

"What do you all say we have a little monster party?" Gameknight shouted.

The villagers cheered, then banged their swords on their leather armor.

"CHANGE ARMOR!" he ordered.

Instantly, all the villages took off their leather tunics and leggings, and donned new, shining iron armor. They banged their swords on the metallic coating, creating a thunderous roar that made the approaching horde hesitate for just an instant before continuing forward.

"Smithy, aren't you going to put on iron armor?" one of the villagers asked in a loud voice, holding out a set for him to use.

Gameknight noticed all the villagers watching him. He smiled.

"No, I don't want that armor," the User-that-is-not-a-user shouted. "I want Herobrine to see me clearly, so that he will know it is Smithy of the Two-Swords that stands before him when he is defeated!"

"Smithy be crazy!" someone shouted, causing the NPCs to laugh aloud as if they didn't care about the approaching mob.

"Let's do this," Gameknight growled as he gripped his swords firmly and waited for the beast to attack.

# CHAPTER 33

# OVERWHELMED

The massive army of monsters stopped far out of bowshot and glared at the defenders. A nervous stillness had settled across the desert, and neither side made a sound. The constant east-to-west breeze made the few dried shrubs rustle in the breeze, causing the leaves to shake like the tail of a rattlesnake just before it strikes.

And then the monsters advanced. The first wave was composed of zombies. The decaying creatures' sorrowful moans and angry growls filled the air as they marched, their shuffling feet kicking up small clouds of dust.

"Archers, take your positions," Gameknight shouted.

The cobblestone towers that sat on either side of the fortified wall filled with warriors. Pointy arrowheads could be seen sticking out from holes in the side of the tower and all along the top. More villagers mounted the walls, standing on catwalks and climbing atop raised platforms behind the wall, and pointed arrows toward their foe.

And then the warriors waited. The monsters seemed to be approaching in slow motion. Fear had a way of doing that, making the terrifying moments in your life feel drawn out and exaggerated. Gameknight had to do something to break the tension.

"Hey, Fencer," Gameknight shouted.

"What?" the NPC replied, confused.

"That one zombie out there . . . he looks kinda like you."

Fencer smiled. Some of the villagers laughed. He understood what the User-that-is-not-a-user was doing.

"Which one?" Fencer replied.

"The decaying one with the ugly scar, the droopy eye, and bald head," Gameknight shouted.

More laughter.

"Bald head?" Fencer shouted, then removed his helmet to show his own head. The sides were ringed with black and gray hair and the top was completely bald. "Who you calling bald? Look at all my hair."

The villagers burst into laughter, the tension easing.

"You know, I feel bad for you, Fencer . . . don't all of you?" Gameknight called out to all the villagers. "All those zombies have the same hairstyle as him . . . you know . . . *bald.*" More laughter. "Everyone, find a bald zombie out there and shoot it with your arrows when it gets near, so our friend here won't feel so bad about his hair style."

"But Smithy," Fencer added with a smile, "they're *all* completely bald."

"Oh, well in that case . . ." Gameknight replied with a grin. "OPEN FIRE!"

The archers released their arrows. Pointed shafts leapt into the air, streaking through the sky in a beautiful arc, then falling upon the green monsters. Sorrowful moans changed to shouts of pain as the arrows found flesh, but the approaching army did not slow. Some of the monsters fell into the many holes placed out in the desert, their heads barely poking up out of the tiny prison. Those behind them just walked over their trapped fellow soldiers, ignoring their plights.

The archers fired again and again, arrows finding their marks, but with so many monsters approaching, the effect was too small to measure. The wave of moaning claws continued forward, unwavering in their desire to reach the NPCs and destroy them.

The growls and moans became louder as they monstrous horde drew closer.

"Swordsmen to the walls!" Gameknight shouted.

Warriors ran to the top of the barricade and waited for the monsters to approach. Their iron swords and new iron armor shone in the light of the morning sun.

"Get ready, they're almost here," Fencer said. "Don't let any get onto the wall!"

As the monsters drew near the wall, the archers were unable to effectively fire at them. Instead, they aimed their projectiles at the monsters farther away from the snarling front line.

And then the army reached the walls. Sharp claws scratched at the stone, hoping to carve through the obstacle. The warriors standing on the barricade knelt and swiped at the monsters with their swords, their blades making zombies flash red with damage. But still they advanced. The creatures in front were forced to the ground, and the ones behind stood on their comrades' fallen bodies. The swordsmen swung their blades, hitting them with all their strength. Monsters flashed red, growling in rage, finally disappearing when their HP went to zero. Fortunately, the swordsmen were able to keep them from creating a living zombie stairway that would have let them reach the top of the wall . . . for now.

Clouds of purple mist formed on the fortified structure; Endermen were teleporting amid the defenders. The dark monsters expected to be attacked, but the User-that-is-not-a-user had trained the villagers well. All of the NPCs glanced away from the Endermen and kept their weapons far from the lanky creatures.

Gameknight smiled. But then he saw one of the soldiers swinging at a zombie head poking up over the wall. A nearby Endermen disappeared in a cloud of lavender, then materialized directly into the path of the blade. The sword dug into the monster's leg, causing it to flash red with damage. With a loud, high-pitched scream, the monster yelled out in pain. The wail caused the other Endermen to screech and become enraged. They began to shake as their mouths fell open, revealing rows of black teeth. Then, as their eyes glowed white with anger, the Endermen attacked.

Soldiers were pummeled in a flurry of dark fists. Their iron armor clanked and groaned under the attack, but was not sufficient to protect the soldiers. NPCs fell under the Endermen attack, taking the pressure off the zombies.

"Fight back-to-back!" Gameknight shouted.

Gripping his swords firmly, he charged to the top of the wall and attacked the nearest Enderman.

The creature took damage before it knew he was there. Then Carver was at his side, axe swinging wildly. Gameknight pressed his back to Carver's as they fought. Endermen that appeared before Gameknight tried to strike him and then teleport to the other side, only to face Carver's axe. Together, they drove the Endermen back, giving the other soldiers time to advance on the zombies.

Arrows were raining down upon them. Glancing out into the desert, Gameknight could see a wave of skeletons approaching, their bony white bodies difficult to see against the pale sand. Most of their arrows were aimed at the NPC archers in the towers, causing the villagers to duck their heads to avoid being hit. This lifted the attack on the zombies, who staggered forward. With the number of zombies reaching the walls getting bigger, the decaying green monsters were close to reaching the top of the wall.

Gameknight stepped back and surveyed the situation.

More zombies were making it to the walls, trampling the monsters ahead of them to reach the top of the cobblestone structure. The skeletons had completely silenced the villager archers, and Endermen were still appearing amid the defenders. Things were not going well.

Suddenly, Gameknight saw a flash of motion amid the monsters. A group of small boys were running through the monster formations, each of them dropping a red-and-white-striped cube behind them. They were weaving between zombies and skeletons, littering the battlefield with them. Fortunately, the monsters were so intent on reaching the defenders on the fortified wall that none of

them paid any attention to the small NPCs sprinting around them.

Gameknight breathed a sigh of relief; it looked
as if Weaver and the other kids were not in danger . . . for now.

A loud clicking sound filled the air. A large group
of spiders had emerged from behind a large sand
dune, mandibles clicking together excitedly as they
surged forward, intent on destruction. They flowed
through the skeleton formation like a shadowy
tide, their black bodies easy to see against the pale
monsters. As they neared the zombies, the fuzzy
monsters veered to the left and approached the cobblestone tower that sat atop a steep sand dune.

Gameknight knew neither the zombies nor the
skeletons would try to assault this tower; the sides of
the sand dune on which it sat were not easily climb-
able. However, the giant arachnids could climb sheer
walls as easily as one could walk along a stone path.

The spiders charged toward the tower, trying to
get around it and gain access to the army's rear. If
they were successful, then Gameknight and all the
NPCs would be trapped between two forces. That
would be bad.

Jumping off the wall, he ran to the Oracle.

"Oracle, we'll need help over there soon,"
Gameknight said.

The old woman nodded her head, then pointed
to the green light-crafter with prickly hair and a tall
light-crafter with brown rough skin. They nodded,
then closed their eyes and concentrated until their
hands began to glow a deep green. At the same
time, the two light-crafters plunged their hands
into the ground just as another light-crafter, this
one with long, stringy green hair, started to help.

Gameknight moved to the left tower and climbed to the top. With his bow out, he began to shoot at the spiders, but he frequently had to duck behind blocks as the skeletons fired up at him. His arrows did not seem to be slowing the fuzzy monsters' advance.

Suddenly, cactuses began popping up out of the ground right in front of the spiders. At the same time, mighty junglewood trees burst into life. Thick, leafy branches extended from the trees, casting dark shadows on the ground. Vines from Vinebrin began to extend down from the branches Treebrin had created. The long, stringy vines began snaking their way across the branches and down the trunks of the trees. When they reached the desert floor, they slithered across the sand like a million green snakes. The vines became entangled in the legs of the spiders, ensnaring them in their verdant mesh, pulling them into the wall of cactus.

Spiders hissed in pain as their bodies flashed red. Some of the monsters were able to cut their way free of the vines and charge forward, only to encounter more prickly cactuses. They moved along the green barrier, looking for a way forward, but Cactusbrin had formed a maze out of the resilient plants. In minutes, the spiders were hopelessly lost, their only option to climb over the walls. When they touched the spines of the cactus, the monsters flashed red again as they took more damage.

Gameknight turned and looked down at the Oracle and smiled. Turning back to the battlefield, the User-that-is-not-a-user peered out from behind a stone block to survey the battle. The villagers on the walls were just barely holding back the monsters. Carver stood at the center of the wall, cleaving through groups of monsters with his axe; none survived who came close to the mighty warrior.

Out in the desert, Gameknight could see Weaver and the others finishing their task. They had placed TNT nearly all throughout the battlefield . . . good.

Suddenly, a loud growl filled the air. Glancing to the large, distant sand dunes, Gameknight watched in shock as another huge group of zombies emerged from hiding. They shuffled across the desert, ignoring the striped blocks and NPC children, their hateful eyes focused on the defenders on the stone tall.

"There must be five hundred in that group," Gameknight mumbled to himself. "How are we going to stop that many?"

He glanced down at the villagers on the walls. They were just barely hanging on as it was—when the new wave of monsters hit the defenses, they would be overwhelmed. There was no way they could hold them back.

Many of the NPCs had now seen the new group of monsters and were shouting alarms, but there was nothing anyone could do. If those zombies reached the walls before they were ready, then they were all doomed.

# CHAPTER 34

# CURTAIN OF FLAMES

ameknight jumped off the tower, landing in a pool of water that cushioned his fall. He then sprinted to the top of the wall and began slashing at the monsters trying to climb over the top. Endermen were still trying to stir up trouble, but with the villagers still fighting back-to-back, the dark creatures were not very effective.

Carver stood tall at the center of the wall. He dared the monsters to approach and frequently stepped back to let them reach the top before cutting them down. The wall all around him was littered with zombie flesh, Ender pearls, and hundreds of glowing balls of XP. He was, singlehandedly, holding the center of their fortifications from the monster advance.

"Gamekn . . . Ahh, I mean Smithy, look," Fencer shouted.

At first, Gameknight thought he was pointing at the new wave of monsters, but then he realized he was really looking at the small NPC on a distant sand dune out in the desert. It was Weaver, and he was standing atop a large hill, waving his iron sword high over his head.

"Grrr . . ." A zombie growled, then attacked Gameknight.

Spinning, he slashed at the monster with his diamond sword. The monster blocked the attack, but it was not ready for the iron blade that came down upon his arm. The monster flashed red with damage. Fear began to fill its cold, dead eyes, but Gameknight999 did not relent. He drove the attack forward, hitting the monster over and over until it disappeared with a *pop*. Glancing up, he could see the rest of the kids gathering around Weaver; their task was complete.

Glancing to his left, he saw Carver using his axe as it was meant to be used—carving through monsters with the ferocity of a hurricane. Zombies and Endermen fell all around him as his shining tool cut through the terrible creatures and cleaved HP from terrifying bodies.

"We can't hold for much longer," Fencer shouted.

Gameknight nodded.

"Do it!" the User-that-is-not-a-user said to Fencer, then turned back and attacked an Enderman.

Fencer moved to a large, open rectangle made of cobblestone. A set of stairs allowed him to climb to the top of the structure that was easily as long as their fortified wall. Fencer then took out a bucket and poured. Lava spilled out of the pail and hit the side of the cobblestone frame, spreading out a few blocks, then fell straight downward into a wide pit. He moved over and poured more lava, letting it fall down the length of the rectangle until molten stone covered the entire rectangle.

"Archers . . . to the lava!" Fencer yelled.

Warriors from the two towers leapt off the tower into pools of water carefully placed around the edge. The water was only one block deep, but it was deep enough for them to fall from the top of the structure without taking any damage.

They all ran behind the lava and stood in a long line.

"Get ready!" Fencer yelled.

The archers notched arrows, then pointed them at different angles so that their shots would be distributed all across the battlefield.

"FIRE!"

The warriors released, and two hundred arrows flew into the curtain of flaming stone. When they emerged, each was on fire, flying through the air like meteors from outer space. The monsters watched as the flaming projectiles came roaring out of the sky and landed among them. Some of the monsters that were hit caught fire, but that was not the offensive's main intent. Instead, many of the arrows found the blocks of TNT left on the desert floor by Weaver and his companions. Instantly, the red-and-white blocks began to blink, then glow bright white.

Suddenly, the TNT exploded, blasting massive holes in the desert as the cubes blossomed into gigantic fiery flowers of destruction. Before the monsters could react, another volley of flaming arrows was flying through the air. More TNT blocks were hit, creating more explosions. With the monsters so tightly packed together, all of them trying to reach the village's defenses, the explosions did incredible damage, wiping out whole companies of zombies and skeletons and spiders.

The archers continued to fire, drawing arrows and releasing them as fast as they could. They didn't bother to aim, sending their arrows out into the air knowing there were so many TNT blocks planted that their shots would likely find a bomb and set it off.

Gameknight finished off the monsters before him, then attacked one of the creatures near Carver. Soon, the advancing monsters were reconsidering their choices, and many of them were fleeing, running back into the desert.

"Now it's our turn to attack!" Gameknight yelled. "FOR MINECRAFT!"

Gameknight and Carver jumped off the wall at the same time, slashing at the creatures still advancing. Suddenly, all of the villagers were leaping forward, chasing down the monsters that were trying to flee, many of them yelling "SMITHY BE CRAZY!" They tore into the enemy, attacking any that turned and faced them. Now it was the monsters that were outnumbered, and they knew it.

The monsters hadn't expected the villagers to attack with such ferocity. Many turned at the sound of their battle cry and just stood there, confused. Herobrine had probably told them that the NPCs were weak and cowardly. Any monster that just stood there was cut down quickly. None were given a chance to attack.

The villagers moved forward like a flood of steel, their swords tearing HP from zombie and skeleton and Enderman bodies. The villagers didn't care what kind of monsters they faced; the sight of Smithy with his two swords slashing a field of devastation into the monsters caused them to fight harder than their tired bodies could have on their own. At times, some of the villagers found themselves facing two monsters at a time, but they were so confident that they didn't even hesitate. Their leader, Smithy of the Two-Swords, was facing dozens with his dual blades; fighting only two or three seemed insignificant.

Off to the left, Gameknight could see the spiders struggling to get free of the cactus obstacle course created by Cactusbrin. Others were using their sharp claws to cut away at the vines that had entangled them. Instead of retreating with the other monsters, the spiders ran off on their own, away from Herobrine's army. Gameknight could see a flash of purple in the distance. It was likely Shaikulud, waiting for her spiders to run to her. He knew it was not over with the spider queen, not yet, but her time would come in the future.

Stopping his charge, Gameknight pulled out blocks of sand and made a small pile. Climbing to the top, he surveyed the battlefield. Most of the monsters had been destroyed by Weaver's TNT. Only a few remained to challenge the villagers. In the distance, he could see the eyes of Herobrine glowing bright with rage as he realized the battle was lost. He would have to signal the retreat for the rest of his monsters, and Herobrine hated to retreat.

They'd done it. They'd won the battle.

He stepped off the pile of stone and moved to Fencer's side. He was about to speak when suddenly, a presence appeared before him. Herobrine materialized four blocks away, glaring at Gameknight999.

"You may have won this battle, blacksmith, but the war is not over," Herobrine growled. "I'll be back, and next time, you won't be so lucky."

"It wasn't luck . . . it was leadership that won the day," Fencer said as he moved to Gameknight's side, his iron sword held at the ready.

Herobrine's eyes glowed bright for just an instant, then he disappeared and materialized on a distant sand dune. The spider queen crawled up the hill and stood at his side, then Erebus appeared next to Shaikulud, his eyes like two blood-red lasers. He reached out and held onto the spider, then the three of them disappeared.

"Fencer, call them all back," Gameknight shouted.

The NPC passed the word to the other villagers. They all began to beckon the warriors back to the village, letting the surviving monsters flee into the desert, leaderless and running for their lives.

Turning back to the hill in the distance, Gameknight saw that Weaver and his friends were gone. Cold fingers of dread gripped his soul for just a moment, then squeezed.

"I hope the monsters didn't get them," Gameknight said with a shudder.

"What?" said a young voice from behind.

Gameknight turned and found Weaver standing behind him, a huge smile plastered on his square face.

"Weaver . . . you did it!" the User-that-is-not-a-user exclaimed.

"What do you mean?" Weaver corrected. "*We* did it!"

"I guess you're right," Gameknight replied.

The warriors all cheered as they gathered around Gameknight999, their weapons held up victoriously in the air. He was about to speak, when some of the villagers began to murmur something.

And then the soldiers parted, allowing someone to approach. It was Carver, his lethal axe in his hands. Gameknight could now hear what they were saying: "The carver of monsters . . . the carver of monsters."

Gameknight smiled, then stepped up to Carver and placed a hand on his shoulder.

"I knew you would find something here to do with that axe," Gameknight said.

The stocky NPC just gave him a satisfied smile.

The User-that-is-not-a-user reached over and lifted Carver's hand and axe in the air, then shouted for all of Minecraft to hear, "CARVER . . . THE CARVER OF MONSTERS!"

The villagers cheered and patted the stocky NPC on the back.

"Sometimes, all you need to do is believe in yourself," Carver said. "You have taught me a great lesson, Smithy. It is something I will never forget."

"Just don't forget about that diamond pickaxe," Gameknight replied, climbing back atop the pile of stone to look at the field of square faces staring up at him.

"We had a great victory here today," Gameknight said.

The villagers cheered. Gameknight waited for their shouts to diminish, then continued.

"But we lost many friends and family members," he added in a solemn tone. Slowly, he raised his hand into the air, fingers spread wide. "We must never forget their sacrifice."

A field of hands sprouted from the NPCs as they all held them high, fingers spread like the petals of a sad flower. Gameknight clenched his hand into a fist as a tiny square tear tumbled down his face. He thought about all the misery and sorrow Herobrine had caused that day, and he grew angry. Squeezing his hand tighter, he tried to crush his grief in his fist until his knuckles popped. Releasing his clenched fist, he lowered his hand down and wiped the tears from his eyes.

"This was a great day, and a sad day," Gameknight said. "But let it be over. It is time to get out of this desert so we can tend to our wounded." He glanced down at Carver. "Perhaps Carver will lead us back to the village."

"CARVER . . . CARVER . . . CARVER," the NPCs chanted.

The stocky NPC stared up at Gameknight and smiled, then marched off back to their defenses, toward home.

## CHAPTER 35

# GOING HOME

Gameknight walked next to the Oracle as they headed southward back to the desert village. The old woman moved slowly, pulling them to the back of the formation. The User-that-is-not-a-user was not concerned. They had scouts all around them and light-crafters walking a dozen paces in front of them. After he'd seen what the strange crafters had done during the battle, he felt very safe with them nearby.

"You know, this isn't over," Gameknight said in a low voice. "Herobrine will not stop until either he is free from this server, or he destroys everything."

"I know," the Oracle replied. "That is the nature of being a virus, to spread and destroy. It is all he knows, therefore it is all he can do."

"You know, far into the future, after the Great Zombie Invasion is finally over, we will meet again," Gameknight said. "And there is something I must tell you."

"No, child, you mustn't tell me now," the old woman said. "Let me ask you something first: Were we successful in the future?"

"Well . . . I guess," Gameknight said. "We finally . . ."

"Don't tell me any more," she insisted. "You see, if you tell me something about the future, then I might change what I did, and the final result could be totally different. If you give me some kind of warning, then I might change a decision I would normally make, causing us to lose our war with Herobrine. It is important that you alter nothing and let the timeline stay as it is, without your insights on the future, so that things will progress naturally to their eventually successful conclusion."

"Well, I guess," Gameknight said.

*I really want to tell you what happens at the jungle temple,* Gameknight thought.

"You know I can hear your thoughts through the fabric of Minecraft, child," the Oracle said.

"Sorry," he replied.

"Mark my words, Gameknight999," she whispered. "Everything must progress normally, without any influence from the future, or the results could be disastrous."

"But I'm here, pretending to be Smithy of the Two-Swords," Gameknight protested softly. "Aren't I already altering the events of history?"

"Perhaps you were *always* Smithy, and this is just part of the natural events," the Oracle said in a soft, grandmotherly voice. "We cannot know for sure until you go back to the future."

*Back to the future,* Gameknight thought. *How am I going to do that?*

If his dad came home and activated the Digitizer, would he get pulled back to the physical world? Would Smithy cease to exist? Or would the timelines just get reset, causing the Great Zombie

Invasion to become history again? Time travel was confusing.

"Don't worry, child," the Oracle said, reassuringly. "I'm sure you will get home when your task here is complete. For now, you must follow this road for a while."

"Roads. Where we're going, we don't need roads," Gameknight said with a smile. It was a quote from one of his favorite movies.

"What are you talking about?" the old woman asked.

"Oh nothing. Just a little joke," he replied.

"Very little, apparently," she said with a smile.

"Smithy . . . Smithy," a voice shouted from the collection of NPCs.

Weaver came running to the back of the formation.

"I'm here," Gameknight shouted.

The young boy ran to him, surrounded by the other young villagers.

"One of the elders said I could be in charge of all TNT and TNT cannons for the village," Weaver said, a bright smile on his square face.

"That's fantastic," Gameknight replied. "Maybe they are beginning to see your value after all, in spite of your age."

"Maybe," he replied.

"Perhaps there is something else you could teach the young boy," the Oracle said.

She stopped walking and closed her eyes. Her hands began to glow a rich forest green. Kneeling, she plunged her hands into the sandstone. Slowly, the emerald light seeped outward until it coalesced at one point. As it grew brighter, a shape began to emerge from the sand, growing taller and taller.

Instantly, Gameknight realized it was another light-crafter.

Sparks of light danced about the creature's hair in every color imaginable. His smock was white with red diagonal stripes running across his chest. Instantly, Gameknight knew the light-crafter's name and thought about his friend far into the future.

"Crafter sure would love to meet you," Gameknight murmured with a smile.

"Who is it?" Weaver asked.

"I believe this is Fireworkbrin," the User-that-is-not-a-user said.

The Oracle smiled and nodded her head.

"I have a few things to teach you now, Weaver," Gameknight said. "I will show it to all of you."

The kids cheered with excitement, then gathered around the blacksmith, all of them talking to him at once. Meanwhile, everyone continued heading toward the desert village, which was just now coming into view. Glancing over his shoulder, Gameknight999 cast the Oracle a smile, then continued on to his new home . . . for now.

# MINECRAFT SEEDS

**B**elow are the Minecraft seeds for the PC version, ver. 1.9. You can create a single player world with these seeds, go to the coordinates, and see the terrain I was looking at while I was writing this book. I've also added these seeds to the Gameknight999 Minecraft server (www.gameknight999.com). If you log into the server (with your parent's permission), go to the survival server. Type the command */warp bookwarps.* This will take you to the book warp room. All the book warps for all of the books have been built here. Go try out these warps for *Attack of the Shadow-Crafters.* I've built

Dragon's Teeth, but at the time that I'm writing this, I haven't built the Great Chasm yet; I'm still trying to figure out how to do that. But hopefully, when these books are printed, the Great Chasm will be there for you to explore. Enjoy!

Chapter 3 – Desert Well:
    686298914, (coordinates: -417, 66, 267)
Chapter 4 – Desert Village:
    1660196624, (coordinates: 116, 68, 157)
Chapter 5 – The Great Chasm:
    on Gameknight999 Minecraft server
Chapter 6 – Birch Forest:
    453275649876, (coordinates: 709, 69, -133)
Chapter 11 – Dragon's Teeth:
    on Gameknight999 Minecraft server

# AVAILABLE NOW FROM MARK CHEVERTON AND SKY PONY PRESS

## THE GAMEKNIGHT999 SERIES
### The world of Minecraft comes to life in this thrilling adventure!

Gameknight999 loved Minecraft, and above all else, he loved to grief—to intentionally ruin the gaming experience for other users.

But when one of his father's inventions teleports him into the game, Gameknight is forced to live out a real-life adventure inside a digital world. What will happen if he's killed? Will he respawn? Die in real life? Stuck in the game, Gameknight discovers Minecraft's best-kept secret, something not even the game's programmers realize: the creatures within the game are alive! He will have to stay one step ahead of the sharp claws of zombies and pointed fangs of spiders, but he'll also have to learn to make friends and work as a team if he has any chance of surviving the Minecraft war his arrival has started.

With deadly endermen, ghasts, and dragons, this action-packed trilogy introduces the heroic Gameknight999 and has proven to be a runaway publishing smash, showing that the Gameknight999 series is the perfect companion for Minecraft fans of all ages.

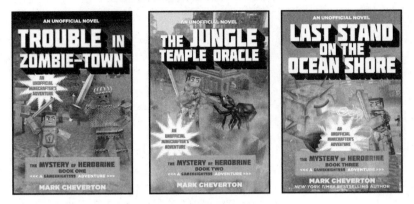

# AVAILABLE NOW FROM MARK CHEVERTON AND SKY PONY PRESS

## HEROBRINE REBORN SERIES

Gameknight999 and his friends and family face Herobrine in the biggest showdown the Overworld has ever seen!

Gameknight999, a former Minecraft griefer, got a big dose of virtual reality when his father's invention teleported him into the game. Living out a dangerous adventure inside a digital world, he discovered that the Minecraft villagers were alive and needed his help to defeat the infamous virus, Herobrine, a diabolical enemy determined to escape into the real world

Gameknight thought Herobrine had finally been stopped once and for all. But the virus proves to be even craftier than anyone could imagine, and his XP begins inhabiting new bodies in an effort to escape. The User-that-is-not-a-user will need the help of not only his Minecraft friends, but his own father, Monkeypants271, as well, if he has any hope of destroying the evil Herobrine once and for all.

Saving Crafter (Book One):
$9.99 paperback • 978-1-5107-0014-7

Destruction of the Overworld (Book Two):
$9.99 paperback • 978-1-5107-0015-4

Gameknight999 vs. Herobrine (Book Three):
$9.99 paperback • 978-1-5107-0010-9

# AVAILABLE NOW FROM MARK CHEVERTON AND SKY PONY PRESS

**THE GREAT ZOMBIE INVASION**
**The Birth of Herobrine: Book One: A Gameknight999 Adventure**
**Can Gameknight999 survive a Minecraft journey one hundred years into the past?**
A freak thunderstorm strikes just as Gameknight999 is activating his father's Digitizer to reenter Minecraft. Sparks flash across his vision as he is sucked into the game . . . and when the smoke clears, he has arrived safely. But it doesn't take long to realize that things in the Overworld are very different. The User-that-is-not-a-user realizes he's accidentally sent himself one hundred years into the past, back to the time of the historic Great Zombie Invasion. None of his friends have even been born yet. But that might be the least of Gameknight999's worries, because traveling back in time also means that the evil virus Herobrine, the scourge of Minecraft, is still alive. . . .

$9.99 paperback • 978–1–5107–0994–2

# EXCERPT FROM HEROBRINE'S WAR

**T**he army ran all through the night and into the morning. Gameknight had them shift frequently from running to walking to sprinting. He knew they couldn't sprint the whole distance to the savanna village; some of Carver's NPCs were still weak from their battle with the ghasts that had destroyed their village. But they moved as fast as they could, with the stronger occasionally scooping up the weaker NPCs and carrying them.

It started to rain just near sunrise. Many of them grumbled about getting wet, but rain meant they were more difficult to see. Unfortunately, the rain only lasted a few hours, and by the time the sun peeked up over the eastern horizon and began repainting the heavens overhead, the rain clouds were gone.

"We are making good time," the Oracle said. She'd been keeping to his side during the evening, her light-crafters always nearby.

"Yes, I agree," Gameknight replied. "I think we'll get to the village before long."

"I see the village!" one of the scouts said.

It was one of Baker's villagers. They'd been sent up ahead and told to climb one of the birch trees. Through the night, they passed from the mega taiga biome, through a grassy hills biome, across frozen rivers, and now finally into a birch forest.

Gameknight sprinted forward and found a tall tree. Placing blocks of dirt under his feet, he built a tiny tower that would give him access to the tree-tops. Once he was on the leafy canopy, he looked in the direction the scout pointed . . . south.

In the distance, he could just barely see structures peeking through the haze of Minecraft. The next biome was savanna, just as predicted, and the village was there, waiting for them. If he squinted and blocked the sunlight from hitting his eyes, he could just barely make out a wall around the village, but that was all he could see.

"I see it, too," Gameknight exclaimed. "Let's head south and get to that village."

But as the User-that-is-not-a-user climbed down from the trees, a chill spread over his body. The faint moaning of zombies could be heard in the direction of the village. And then the chuckles of Endermen added to the sound, causing tiny square goose bumps to form on his arms and neck.

Quickly, he ran back up to the treetops, then gasped in shock at what he saw. Monsters were appearing between his army and the savanna village. Endermen were teleporting them into position, then disappearing in clouds of purple mist, only to reappear again with more snarling creatures in tow. As he watched, hundreds of monsters materialized and then stood next to each other, zombies, skeletons, and Endermen forming a lethal picket fence, blocking them from the salvation of the village.

Icicles of fear stabbed at Gameknight's soul as he descended from the treetops. By now, everyone in the army could hear the monsters.

"What is it?" Carver asked.

"Monsters," Gameknight replied.

"You think?" Baker added.

"They've blocked us off from the savanna village," Gameknight explained. "If we head south, it will mean a direct battle with them. And with their numbers, I don't think we can win that fight."

"Maybe we can go back and sneak around them," Weaver suggested.

Just as Gameknight was about to answer, a clicking sound percolated through the forest from behind. It was like a million crickets were out there among the trees. He could tell from the volume that they weren't close, but there were a lot of them, and they were probably coming fast.

Everyone heard the spiders and turned to face Gameknight999, expecting him to say or do something that would make everything OK. But he had nothing to say; there were two armies closing in on them and they were totally exposed, with no village walls to hide behind.

Feline cries then drifted to them from the north.

"Ghasts," Gameknight moaned. "What next . . . the Ender dragon?"

"There's a dragon?" Weaver exclaimed, his eyes wide with fear.

"No, there's no dragon, just a lot of monsters," the User-that-is-not-a-user replied.

Another ghast screeched from the north. Anxious eyes glanced toward the sound; none of them wanted to face the ghasts again, especially out here in the open.

"It seems we have no choice," Gameknight said. "The only direction we can go is west."

"Then let's get moving," Carver said in a loud, commanding voice. "Archers to the outside of the formation. Elderly to the center. If anyone needs help running, let someone know and you'll be carried. LET'S GO!"

The army, buoyed by Carver's confidence, started running to the west. They emerged from the birch forest and began moving across the savanna, the hot, dry air hammering into them as if they were standing before a furnace. But this time no one complained—hot, dry air was preferable to claws and fangs.

Acacia trees, each bent and twisted into a different shape, dotted the landscape. They were the only things visible around them, but as they ran over the large, rolling hills, Gameknight became nervous.

*We're easy to see on the hilltops*, he thought. *We need to be more careful.*

Motioning to the big NPC, he had Carver lead the army around the hills instead of over, in hopes that the monsters would lose track of where they were.

Suddenly, a group of spiders jumped out from a hole in the ground, their black bodies scurrying over the savanna hill. They charged at the villagers, their sharp mandibles clicking together as their eyes glowed bright red. Without thinking, Gameknight drew his two swords and attacked.

Sprinting to the lead spider, he leapt high into the air, then landed on the beast, smashing it with his swords. The monster squealed in pain and tried to knock him off, but Gameknight kept attacking until the monster disappeared with a *pop*.

There were only five of them left. Turning to the next one, he slashed at it as he ran past, then shot through their formation and attacked from the rear. By know, Carver and the other swordsmen had formed a line of armor and were pushing forward. The spider claws were scratching at the metallic plating, causing damage, but as they focused in the warriors before them, Gameknight attacked from the rear. He slashed and poked with his swords, tearing at their HP as he sped by. Not bothering to stand and fight them one at a time, the User-that-is-not-a-user ran past and did small amounts of damage with each pass, just like in his dad's favorite game, Wing Commander. Hit and run, that's what he did, zipping past the fuzzy monsters with his swords spinning like a razor-sharp tornado. By the time the monsters reached Carver and his warriors, they had little HP left and were quickly destroyed.

"SMITHY!" the warriors chanted as he stepped through the battlefield, glowing balls of XP flowing into his feet.

Many of the NPCs had stopped during the attack. Those from Baker's village were shocked at the ferocity of Gameknight's attack, not to mention his two-sword fighting tactics.

"They should have known not to mess with Smithy of the Two-Swords," Weaver said, pride filling his voice. More villagers cheered, their shouts drowning out the clicking of the massive spider army that was still moving through the forest.

"SMITHY!" they shouted again.

"That doesn't matter right now," Gameknight said. "We don't stop . . . we keep going. That horde of spiders back there will not be so easily overcome."

The army kept running. It was Gameknight's plan that they'd go far enough to the west that they could swing around the monster army, and sneak into the village. But to do that, they had to move faster than Herobrine expected. And for that to happen . . . they had to run!

Suddenly, an Enderman appeared behind the army with two skeletons in his arms. The creature disappeared, then reappeared with more of the pale bony monsters. The skeletons instantly began firing at the villagers, their arrows streaking through the air. Some bounced off armored bodies while other pointed shafts found flesh.

Archers formed a line at the rear of the army and returned fire. At the same time, Carver and a group of warriors moved around a hill and surprised them from behind. Carver's diamond pickaxe carved through the monsters, cleaving multiple skeletons with a single swing. In seconds, the bony monsters were destroyed.

"I don't like this," Gameknight said.

"Why?" Weaver asked.

"Those attacks aren't meant to do any damage. They're just to keep pushing us to the west," Gameknight said.

"But we won every battle," Baker said. "Those monsters didn't have a chance."

"That's just it," Gameknight replied. "They never had a chance. Those skeletons and spiders were completely outnumbered and they knew it, but they attacked anyway."

"The skeletons didn't seem too excited about that battle," Carver said as he returned to the army with his squad of swordsmen and swordswomen. "They kept looking to the south when we attacked. It was as if they were expecting reinforcements, but obviously, none ever came."

"You see, Herobrine is sacrificing these creatures to keep us going west," the User-that-is-not-a-user complained. "The questions is . . . why?"

"I'm not sure we have much choice," Weaver said, pointing to the south.

Gameknight turned and looked in that direction. The line of monsters still stood just on the horizon, their bodies forming a multicolored line along the savanna. The sun was now high in the sky and beat relentlessly down upon the villagers, making the monsters easy to see.

"Behind us!" someone shouted.

Gameknight turned to the east. Fuzzy black spiders could be seen emerging onto the savanna, cresting over a distant hill and flowing over the acacia trees as if they were twigs in a raging river. More spiders appeared to the north; not as many as those to the east, but there was no way the villagers could head for the smaller group without the larger catching them.

"It seems we have no choice," Baker said, her bright blue eyes filled with worry. "Herobrine seems insistent we continue to the west."

"I think you're right," Gameknight replied. "If we are going to be pushed to the west, let's see if we can get there before their trap is ready. Now, what we need is speed. COME ON, EVERYONE!"

The warriors beat their swords on their chests as they began to sprint to the west, the sun now at its zenith. Dashing across the savanna, the army took the two monster armies by surprise and quickly left them far behind. Gameknight led them around hills and in shallow ravines whenever possible, keeping their position hidden from their pursuers. It was a hard run, with the hot savanna desert sun beating down upon them, but fortunately, clouds were slowly moving in from the east. They all knew the blazing yellow square overhead would soon be blocked and they'd get at least a small amount of relief from the sweltering temperature. After ten minutes of running, Gameknight slowed to a walk and looked back along their path. No monsters were visible anywhere . . . perfect.

"Since we can't see them, they can't see us," Gameknight said.

More clouds moved in, dropping the temperature even more. Many of the villagers seemed relieved with the cool air finally hitting their sweaty bodies, some smiling for the first time since they had left the birch forest.

Gameknight looked around and thought this part of the savanna looked familiar. It reminded him of Herder, his friend from the future, as well as Cobbler, the young boy whose village was taken by the zombie king. It seem so long ago when that had occurred, yet it had to wait for a hundred years before it could happen again . . . strange. Then he realized it: the savanna village to the south was the one Cobbler had taken them too, but he couldn't remember why. There was a river just on the other side of the next hill, and . . . something else, he couldn't quite recall.

"We need to do what Herobrine doesn't expect," Gameknight said as he brought his attention back to the moment. He glanced at Baker and Carver, who were now running side-by-side. "We're going to start veering to the north in hopes of attacking that small group of spiders."

The two leaders smiled and nodded their blocky heads.

But just as they started to head northward, a hideous catlike yowl filled the air. Gameknight glanced around, looking to see if it came from behind. The sound came again, this time with an evil baby-like cry on top of the feline howl.

The noise wasn't coming from behind or from the north or south. It was coming from straight overhead. Directly above them, a massive cluster of ghasts lowered down from a strange-looking cloud. They all had a hateful, evil look to them, the innocent babe-like faces completely erased and replaced with the terrifying look of a nightmare.

"OINK, OINK!" Wilbur squealed as the monsters began forming fireballs beneath their tentacles.

"GHASTS!" Weaver yelled as he scooped up the pig and began to run.

And as Gameknight looked up, he saw three massive fireballs heading straight for him. Fear pulsed through every nerve in his body as he watched the flaming balls of death descend down upon him, and all he could do was stand there and wait for his doom.

COMING SOON:
**HEROBRINE'S WAR:**
**THE BIRTH OF HEROBRINE BOOK THREE**